Hold Up Your Heads, Girls!

Annie H. Ryder

Contents

INTRODUCTION. 7

I. HOW TO TALK. 11

II. HOW TO GET ACQUAINTED WITH NATURE. 21

III. HOW TO MAKE THE MOST OF WORK. 31

IV. WHAT CAN I DO?. 36

V. WHAT TO STUDY. 45

VI. ENGLISH LITERATURE AND OTHER STUDIES. 52

VII. THE COMMONPLACE. 61

VIII. MOODS. 69

IX. WOMANLINESS. 76

X. GIRLS AND THEIR FRIENDS. 85

XI. YOUTHS AND MAIDENS. 94

HOLD UP YOUR HEADS, GIRLS!

BY

Annie H. Ryder

To My Girls Everywhere.

INTRODUCTION.

When we make an object with our hands, we frequently notice that the most care is needed as we near its completion. A false stroke of the brush will change an angel into a demon, a misguided blow of the mallet will shiver the statue into fragments: so, in the work which attempts to form a noble womanhood, all the efforts of years of training will be marred or rendered ineffectual, if the right influence, proper occupation, and wholesome encouragement are not given to a girl in the period which borders on womanhood. We wait for the rose to open; but if we allow the atmosphere to become impure, or otherwise prevent its development, its life will stagnate, it will refuse to give out odor, and the world will lose that beauty it might have enjoyed.

Susceptible as girls are, vigorous, affectionate, cheerful and aspiring, if they are deprived suddenly of good influence and encouragement, the very conditions of their growth will be removed, and they, like the rose, will shut their lives within their lives.

There is no time in a girl's life so neglected, and yet so dependent upon sympathy, as that when she is first thrown upon her own efforts. Too old to be any longer led, she is not old enough to be left without guidance. This time usually comes when she has finished the ordinary school course and finds herself, all at once, waiting, either for an entrance into what is called society, or for an opportunity to earn her living.

There is a certain lightness of heart, carelessness, *abandon*, maybe, about girls while they are still in school, which is both delightful and natural, however provoking to teachers. Every thing is very bright now; and if the girl learns her lessons, is obedient, and tries to think, she believes that somehow things will all come around right with time. All at once she is confounded. She awakes in the morning, and finds that school does not keep to-day,--no, nor to-morrow! What is to be done? Going and coming, which get to be more going and coming; dish-washing, which daily increases into dish-washing; or *ennui*, which degenerates into melancholy, ensue. Life is not what the school-girl supposed. Six months of it make her older than a whole school-year.

Girls look upon graduation day as a grand portal through which they are to enter into a palace glistening with splendor; but, lo! when they reach that portal, they see only a very low gate-way, while a hedge, thorny and high, shuts out the palace. How to get through? Rather, how are their elders to make them see that, with the patience and energy of the prince in the story, they can cause the hedge to turn to roses, and open wide before them?

A girl needs, first of all, encouragement. She should not be told what things are to oppose her, if she has ambition to excel in a certain direction, but what things are to help her to attain her purpose. She wants praise, but not flattery. A girl knows when she is flattered sooner than a boy. If conceit is engendered from praise, that will do no harm. Time will destroy conceit, if a girl has much to do with sensible people and sensible books.

A girl needs to be trusted. Nothing will be more efficacious than making her feel of certain importance and usefulness to others. It is evident she wants sympathy in her endeavors and disappointments. I do not mean that she should be indulged, or that she should not be made to work out her own salvation; but that she should realize that, if she tries, some one will know and bless her, and if she stumbles, some one will help her up again. Just as truly should she know that, if she is careless of endeavor or negligent of her days, she will meet with disparagement and punishment.

It is most necessary for a girl to have a motive placed before her, that she may bring out whatever undeveloped faculties may be latent within her. This motive may be a comparatively slight one,--no more than the training of a window-garden, the collecting of newspaper slips, or the making of bread; but, if she does her particular work better than others, she will attain a certain degree of superiority, and her time has, for her, been as profitably filled as that which another person devotes to a larger work. By motive, let me repeat, I mean something given a girl to do which shall be especially her work: not always an ambitious one,--a desire to shine in society, letters, or the arts,--but something just for herself, with its own rewards.

How much more numerous the motives which can be given an American girl than one who lives on foreign soil! Look at the German girl, for example. Her country arbitrarily divides its people into high and low. The peasant maiden has so long stayed one side of the barrier, she thinks she always must; so, with her scanty loaf of black bread near her on the ground, she leans against a tree, knits her stocking, and tends the flock. When night comes she goes home to her rude stone cottage, lifts a prayer to the Virgin, if she is an Austrian, and one for the king. Her mind never strays beyond the village gate. The more fortunate girls in towns and cities receive the allotted years of study in the schools, and when these end at fifteen, about the time of confirmation, the girls are put into families away from home to get a year's experience in domestic matters. Then they marry, and obediently follow the commands of their husbands.

It may be thought that a society girl needs no incentives to a right use of time and privileges, but she most certainly does. Her responsibility is great: she will either sway a circle or a household. Her influence will as surely affect her associates as did the influence of those celebrated French women whose *salons* were the places where battles were fought and decisive moments gained. Society is in great need of women: it always will be. Now this period of young womanhood is precisely the time for cultivating those principles which will later be most helpful to society.

Surely, for those who are to bear more heavily the weight of life, who are to work as they wish not; in fact, in a way against which all but principle struggles,--certainly, for these, there is every need of motive. This class increases daily, and the discouragement and distrust of its members grow with sad rapidity.

Girls, girls everywhere,--my girls,--do not think I mean to flatter you! Do not think I mean to praise you more highly than I ought! I simply want you to know your own capabilities, and to realize that much, very much, depends upon every one of you. How much there is for you to do! You are frank and honest now, or ought to be; you have not learned to imitate the falseness of so-called proprieties. It is fully possible to keep young, genuine, girlish even, and at the same time to be womanly. The world is not sunshiny enough; there are too many November days in the year: bring fairer weather and fresh June mornings.

You are not awkward, even if you have not learned just how to be graceful; you are not useless, though you have not yet acquired all the knowledge of the kitchen, laundry, and sewing-room; nor are you unprofitable because you do not now earn the so many dollars a week you will sometime gain. There is large hope of you, even when you forget yourselves in the use of fashionable slang, because your minds and hearts are open to receive kind warnings, and to learn to despise such terms as mar the beauty of easy, delicate speech.

You want courage and physical strength outside of your lively affections. You want wisdom and long training in the use of books. You need to be occupied, to be active in brain and heart and hand; busied even with more than the duties assigned you; occupied in times of rest as well as in times of labor.

You should see more and feel no less. Indeed, the power of observation is most cultivating and most easily developed.

You ought to be more familiar with Nature,--the sky, and trees, and fields; not always to have a scientific knowledge of it, but a certain familiarity, so that you may ever be surrounded by a glorious company of friends. You need to know the value of literature, and to adorn yourselves with the graces of conversation.

Those qualities which contribute most to womanhood and character you should be most eager to make your own.

May I talk with you about such subjects as may suggest ways of educating your minds, of benefiting your bodies, and of helping, in some little measure, towards that growth of soul which should be the aim of all instruction?

I.
HOW TO TALK.

I saw a group of girls the other day bidding one another good-by after a year together at boarding-school. It was the merriest, most sparkling, set of people!--girls in every sense!--bobbing about, kissing, tuning their voices in all sorts of keys, with apparently not one care nor the shadow of an unpleasant memory! How I longed to get right in among them, and be hugged with the rest! though the hugging came along with armfuls of umbrellas, bags, hats, rackets, and whatever else would not go into the last inch of trunk. Pretty dresses, jaunty hats, tidy gloves and boots they wore; but better than these were their bright, honest faces, and the hearty words they spoke, Cheerfulness seemed to gush out in the wildest hilarity. How they talked with their tongues, and their eyes, and their hands! Enthusiasm sent their words racing after each other into sentences which had no beginning and no end.

Though you might never guess it, from the confusion of their language, these girls were practising some of the first principles in the art of conversation, without, indeed, being conscious of it. They were sincere and in earnest.

A girl is born to be a readier talker than a boy. She is usually less positive; and, as she has more animation, more spontaneity, more feeling, she talks much more. But somehow these natural gifts for talking are not cultivated by her as they should be: sometimes they are wholly disregarded. In a few years those very girls, who talked so fluently and engrossingly, will be sitting in corners trying to patch sentences together into what is called conversation.

Now, my dear girls, the importance of this art of talking is so great that. I should almost say any other art you may acquire cannot be compared with it; in fact, it is something so necessary to us that persons who are lacking in it stand in great danger of being metaphorically swallowed by the words of such individuals as know the cunning uses of language. Loosen some persons' tongues, and, no matter what sacrifices of character, of friendship, of good training, they have to make, they will reach the goal of their endeavor, and drive every one else into a corner. The power of eloquence and persuasion is mightier than any two-edged sword, and cuts down enemies like the sickle before the harvest. Go never so determined to remain unconvinced by certain talkers, and, before their eloquence ceases, you are enemies to yourselves, and wonder you never thought their way before.

Do not let me misguide you, however. Though you may be deceived by words, finding yourselves utterly incapable of replying to argument, still the joys you receive from the talks of certain well-minded persons are far greater than any danger I have implied.

What is it which makes some persons using very simple words say them so they drop like manna into hungry minds and hearts, or electrify with grand ideas and moving suggestions? Some will answer that it is brightness of intellect, and a keenness of insight added to profound thoughtfulness. I believe this in a large measure, though, if it were always true, we should oftener be able to understand certain full-mouthed speakers, deep thinkers, and philosophers. They do any thing but electrify, and suggest little more than sleep and weariness. Others will reply that successful talking is the effect of personal magnetism. That may be true to a slight degree. When certain strangers enter the room, we sometimes realize at once that it will be extremely difficult to say any more than yes or no to them; while others, previously unknown to us, may come in and draw out thoughts from us in rapid succession,--thoughts we hardly knew we were capable of expressing. But I would define a large part of the personal magnetism used in talking as an honest compound of heartiness, thoughtfulness, and sympathy.

Conversation does not demand that we should always be vivacious, sparkling, witty, fanciful, or even that we should use beautiful language; but good talk does ask for heart and interest. Put your heart into what you have to say: put your interest into it, and your conscience will be awakened, your zeal will be aroused; then you will compel attention, and set others thinking also. De Quincy writes, "From the heart, from an interest of love or hatred, of hope or care, springs all permanent eloquence; and the elastic spring of conversation is gone if the talker is a mere showy man of talent, pulling at an oar which he detests."

These things being true, it seems to me that character is the first requirement in the art of conversation. I take it for granted that every girl can, with perseverance, acquire a fluent use of words; for this depends mainly on practice: so I shall try to indicate those qualities which lie back of the words, and which give life to them. Even the nature of a talk will have its source in character, and to character it will return. Whatever chance or circumstance brings about a conversation, it will generally lead to such expressions of ideas as will show the dispositions of the conversers.

Just here, girls, let me remark, that, if by any slang or catch words you thoughtlessly express yourselves, the danger is, your character will be misunderstood, and your pure hearts but merry minds will be censured for what is not in them. Depend upon it, your own personality will be inferred from what you say, hence the value of utter sincerity in what you talk.

Naturally, we are led to think about courtesy and good manners as requirements in the art of talking. Have you not met certain men and women who, when they opened their mouths to speak to you, conferred a favor on you? and, when they spoke, have you not felt the benediction descending on your heads? I have. They were not always scholars, nor were they great people, nor rich people, but *mannered* people. Such persons used their words as if they expected words from you, for which they would be grateful. They did not monopolize conversation, neither did they frequently interrupt; but when they had a suggestion to offer, opportunity being afforded, they spoke honestly, though politely, their good sound thoughts,-- ideas which frequently destroyed the evil of gossip or impatiently uttered remarks.

Conversation does not depend upon rapidity of speech, as certain impulsive persons seem to think. I acknowledge that much of the interruption in conversation, and much of the monopoly, and a large number of the quick, almost angry words, result from eagerness rather than conceit or selfishness. If one cannot be animated without rapid speech, let him talk fast. It is a bad practice, however, even in the ablest talkers.

One can have opinions, and yet not use them to knock down one's opponents who have had no chance to arm against one. Do not be ungenerous, girls, selfish, in talking. Allow that some one else may have ideas as good as yours. George Eliot says, in "Daniel Deronda," "I cannot bear people to keep their minds bottled up for the sake of letting them off with a pop." That is not conversation: it is a selfish display of a few treasured maxims or witticisms or opinions.

If courtesy, deference, patience, and generosity are needed to talk well, then certainly sympathy is necessary. A woman who has no comfortable word for her sister woman had better talk to the wall. But I need not reproach girls for lack of sympathy, nor for lack of interest in the girls they meet. Their confidence in new friends is so absolute; their desire to receive sympathy, as well as to give it, is so great, that they frequently impart their whole lists of secrets to the bosoms of others whom they have not known a month. Now a more careful use of sympathy and confidence will induce not only good manners but good talk. It will tell you how to avoid such subjects as would give rise to unpleasant, even quarrelsome, talk. It will show you when you have talked too long with one person in a mixed company, and when you are wounding the feelings of another by paying no regard to her.

Impartial treatment of those we meet in society is certainly very charming. We say it is a great accomplishment to be able to speak a pleasant word to the neighbor on the right, and a different, though equally expressive, one to the friend on the left. Mary likes books, Sallie prefers society, Ruth enjoys housekeeping, Margaret is fond of music. Then why not ask Mary if she has noticed the beautiful woodcuts in the last Harper's, or seen the new edition of Hawthorne? Why not inquire of Sallie about the last matinee and the last hop? Why not ask Ruth how she made those delicious rolls, and how she prepared the coffee, or how she manages to make her room look so cheerful and cosey? And why not make Margaret give you her opinion of Wagner or of Beethoven?

I cannot dwell too long on the necessity of that adaptability to others which a kind and sympathetic heart will always strive for in conversation. Suppose you do not know the group amidst which you are seated in a drawing-room, and it is expected you will all become acquainted? Well, if it must be, say something to Miss Brown about yesterday's storm or today's sunshine; something to Miss Eliot about the kindness of your hostess, who is entertaining her friends in her usual hospitable manner, with a word to each just suited to the individual addressed; and something to Mrs. Hammerton about the pleasant surroundings,--a picture near you, a book, a vase of exquisite form.

But suppose you are to talk with a gentleman? Why, begin with just such remarks as you would use to a sensible girl; and, if he does not seem to care for them, turn his attention to the world of his own affairs,--to the street and the office. A man often takes pleasure in giving information about matters of great public interest of which so many girls are ignorant. After you have passed a few remarks about the last election, or the new town-hall, you will probably find out what he prefers to discuss, and then you can easily entertain him, and be entertained in return. I think that most men are quite as fond of general topics in conversation as women are; and I fail to see the necessity of introducing different subjects for gentlemen than for ladies,--I mean when both young men and young women appreciate what it is to be gentlemen and ladies.

Girls, why do so many of you indulge in so much smaller talk with men than with women? Because it is expected of you? Only by a few, and they make themselves very absurd by always trying to say nonsensical things to you. Men of this sort appear to have an impression that you are still children amused with a Jack-in-the-box which springs up in a very conceited hobgoblin way. Everybody likes a joke, and at times feels a childlike pleasure in speaking nonsense; but, believe me, sense is much more attractive in conversation.

Discretion in conversation really implies a peculiar tact of woman, a kind of cleverness, not so frequently found in men, and very seldom met with in boys. When a woman sees her guests are led by a monopolizer along unsafe channels of thought, she can easily, by that happy faculty of hers, bring them back again where all will run smoothly. She can change the subject by some little remark irrelevant to it. Perhaps adaptability comes from discretion. When you are talking with Englishmen,--well, do not talk quite as Englishmen do, though they may be perfectly sincere; but talk as Americans talk. Say *a* the way they do in Boston, or wherever else you may belong: stick to your own town's forms of speech so long as they are reasonable. Above all things, do not ape the peculiar pronunciations of certain individuals. Affectation, imitation in talk, is ruinous. Be yourselves! Girls and boys are not themselves as much as they ought to be.

Being honest, still adapt yourselves to new people as you would to new scenes: talk with the Englishman on such subjects as he prefers. When you are speaking with honest country people about the beauty of their fields, do not talk about "Flora spreading her fragrant mantle on the superficies of the earth, and bespangling the verdant grass with her beauteous adornments." Use baby talk to babies; kind and simple words to the aged; a good, round, cheerful word to the girls, almost slang,--though no, not quite that! Make the grocer feel you have an interest in groceries; the seamstress an interest in sewing, as of course you have; and the doctor an interest in sickness. In fact, make each one with whom you come in contact realize that you care for him and what he specially does. Just put yourselves into the places of others, and the words will take care of themselves.

The intellect is not such a supreme factor in conversation as the points of character I have so far named. Mr. Mathews, in his "Great Conversers," writes, "The character has as much to do with the colloquial power as has the intellect; the temperament, feelings, and animal spirits even more, perhaps, than the mental gifts." I add this remark from De Quincy: "More will be done for the benefit of conversation by the simple magic of good manners (that is, chiefly by a system of forbearance) applied to the besetting vices of social intercourse than ever *was* or *can* be done by all varieties of intellectual power assembled upon the same arena."

But there are certain things the mind must do in connection with the disposition. Concentrating the thoughts is one of these things,--very hard for young or old to acquire. Persons resort to very queer methods to obtain it,--some scratch their heads, others rub their chins. I have seen a public speaker try to wreak thoughts out of a watch-chain. Another jerked at the rear pockets of his swallow-tailed coat to pick out a thought there. You know the story Walter Scott tells about the head boy? He always fumbled over a particular button when he recited; so, one day, the button being furtively removed by Walter, the boy became abstracted, and Scott passed above him. Madame De Stael, as she talked, twisted a bit of paper, or rolled a leaf between her fingers. (Some have attributed this to her vanity, as she had very beautiful hands.) I believe friends came to note her necessity, and supplied her with leaves. Well, do what you will that is harmless, if it but serve to pin your attention right down to the matter before you.

The great conversers of literature are wrongly called so. Set topics do not often lead to genuine conversation, and those who occupy the time by delivering their ideas on given subjects are really lecturers. Johnson as well as Coleridge talked right on while all the rest sat and listened.

Conversation that is real implies give and take. We do not talk to illuminate the minds of others only, but to get their ideas also. And, don't you see, we never quite know what our own thoughts are till we come to try to make them clear to others? "Intercourse is, after all, man's best teacher. 'Know thyself is an excellent maxim; but even self- knowledge cannot be perfected in closets and cloisters."[1] Three or four expressing ideas on the same subject give one a larger range of thoughts, make one more liberal and less obstinate.

If you care for a girl's opinion because it is just like yours, maybe it is her sympathy you are after and not her opinion. An interchange of ideas sometimes leads to discussion, and that is admirable for the growth of mind, provided it does not degenerate into dispute.

It is not necessary that conversation should roll around a given point. I think that is the most entertaining, restful, and real talk which is the most roving. You may begin in Portland and end in San Francisco. You may start talking about preserving peaches, and halt on the latest sensation. It is often very amusing to trace the line of such converse: it moves in a zigzag course, and terminates many miles out of the original direction. By this discursiveness I do not mean gossip. Of course talk of that kind has no good part in conversation: it is the slave of ignorance and bad character. I might, however, differ from some as to what gossip is,--whether there may not be certain kinds of talk miscalled gossip. I am quite sure that criticising the misfortunes of others, and watching a chance for dilating upon their lot, with your neighbors on the next doorstep, would come under the head of worse than gossip. It might be well to distinguish between gossip and scandal: the one is goodness adulterated; the other is evil unmixed.

Good conversation is the mark of highest culture. That is why, in spite of shabby dresses, unbanged hair, tremendous mouths, and large noses, some persons are purely delightful. We have seen that this is so, yet have not added that something lies in the voice as well as in the manners and words of such people. From nervousness, and other causes which I have not been able to trace, girls are apt to pitch their voices too high, as though they thought to be better able to speak distinctly. A gruff, mannish voice is worse than a piping, shrill tone in a woman; but fulness of tone prevents no melody, and this comes from a medium pitch. In the very modulations of the voice are detected excellence and refinement. The human voice, in its sounds

---

1   Mathews.

and accents, is a record of character: trust it as the key-board of the human being.

May I remind you here, girls, of the harm arising from loud talk in public places? How many times do we suffer annoyance from the noisy voice in the car, the station, or on the street! How bold and immodest such tones are! Some persons seem to think the public is not to be regarded, and that it has no right to criticism. They appear to believe that a train is no different than an open field, where the voice needs no restraint, and where manners are not the most refined. They treat the passengers with as little care as they do the cars; for, while they make a waste-basket of the latter, they regard the former as so many brazen images to be stared at *ad libitum*. Passengers have ears, though they themselves be removed from the talkers by the distance of a seat or two.

Now about the words you use, girls. I fully realize the expressiveness of slang and the convenience of exaggeration. But if a peach pie is almost "divine," and the Hudson River "awfully lovely," what can be said of the New Testament and Niagara Falls? What is to become of the poor innocent words in the English language which mean only delicious and beautiful? By a girl's words know her; but, oh! never by the slang she uses. This use of slang is really a serious matter. Honest words are so mis-construed, and propriety in the employment of them so injured,--phrases are capable of so many interpretations,--that even serious people use slang in a very pathetic way without ever knowing the words are slang. Girls not only hurt themselves, but go to work to defame the very English language and the people who speak English.

When a young woman, who makes much pretension to fine manners and an elegant education, takes the steam-car for a rostrum, and exclaims about her French teacher as "awfully funny but awfully horrid, don't you know; awfully lovely some-times, but awfully awful at others!" we wonder why she gives so much attention to French when her English vocabulary seems to have reduced itself to the scanty proportions of one word. Oh, I know how pertinent certain kinds of slang are! I acknowledge that a few peculiar expressions convey ideas more emphatically than whole pages of classical English.

The dangers from the habitual use of slang cannot be too strongly presented. Imagine a girl of the period versed in the loose expressions of the day. She goes away; but, after an absence of five years in a country where she hears little except in a foreign tongue, she returns, and with her comes her slang. How common, how witless, her talk appears! Her slang has long since gone out of fashion. The best of English never changes its style.

Girls, especially very young girls, must have their secret signs, their language of nods and becks and shrugs; but young ladies who have outgrown "eni, meni, moni, mi; husca, lina, bona, stri," ought to outgrow signs which are suggestive of coarse, rude acts, and which, with the slang expressions that accompany them, have often originated in some theatre of questionable character.

The responsibility rests with you, girls, to stop this increasing use of slang, and of words of double meaning. I say you can prevent it because you are so much regarded. Your influence is wide, wider than you suppose. If you do not cease speaking slang, your younger sisters will not, your friends and acquaintances may not. More than this: if you use coarse words, or those which may be interpreted in various ways, then coarse manners will soon follow coarse tones, and a general swaggering and lawlessness. My dear girls, I am only prophesying what will be if no prevention is employed. Surely you will give no cause for censure, if you seriously think about this matter.

It is a part of youthful exuberance to exaggerate. Children always want a thing as long as "from here to Jerusalem," and stretch their tiny arms out till they nearly fall backwards, trying to make an inch as long as a mile. But, ***cave canem***! the fault of exaggerating once powerful over you, not only the bounds of the English language are leapt, but truth is unconsciously set at nought. We always allow for the words of some persons, for with them a scratch is a wound; a wind, a hurricane; one dollar, a thousand; and all they do in life, a big, big bluster. The only way to bring back English to a state of purity--for it has been outraged by slang, imitation, technical expressions, a straining after long words, and a regular system of exaggeration--is to speak simple words, using all necessary force and emphasis in the voice instead of in the number of syllables, saying what you mean by just the words that will convey the meaning. Of course the dictionary must be frequently used. There is no help so sure as that which it affords to one who would use language properly.

Do not be troubled if you hesitate in conversation, and cannot immediately find the proper word. Search in your mind till you get the expression, then next time it will come more rapidly. One of the best ways to increase fluency of speech is to avoid repetition of words as much as possible. Turn the name of an object or of an idea into a phrase, or substitute a synonym, and in this way you add variety and words to your vocabulary. Do not use foreign words when English will do as well. There are times when it will not, though it is a very copious language. Never think English inferior. Hear its music in Tennyson and Longfellow, De Quincey and Ruskin. See its beauty in the pages of Hawthorne and Irving. Do not use technical terms with those unacquainted with science or art. It shows a lack of good sense.

I want once more to insist on the value of good conversation, more particularly because of its suggestiveness. I believe there are few things really great and good which have not this power of suggestion. The picture is not wonderful that can be appreciated at a glance, the book is not remarkable which will not bear a second reading, music is not good unless it awakes harmonies, a thought is not valuable unless it suggests another thought.

The graces of conversation none can wear as well as woman. They are most becoming to you, my dear girls,--even brighter and richer and dearer than any jewels with which you may adorn yourselves. They consist mostly of pleasant, well-chosen words, sympathetic, hearty tones, sprightliness, and certain winsome modulations of voice.

When every other accomplishment fails to entertain, there is always left the resource of good talk, pleasing to old and young. We cannot sit at Luther's table, and hear him utter life-giving words, "If a man could make a single rose, we should give him an empire; yet roses, and flowers no less beautiful, are scattered in profusion over the world, and no one regards them." We cannot listen to Coleridge, "with his head among the clouds." We, alas! cannot even catch the energetic flash of Margaret Fuller's words. But every one of us can improve her conversation by persevering effort in the ways indicated, and can listen still to the best of talk.

Somewhere Emerson writes, "Wise, cultivated, genial conversation is the last flower of civilization, and the best result which life has to offer us,--a cup for the gods, which has no repentance."

II.
HOW TO GET ACQUAINTED WITH NATURE.

My dear girls, I want to talk to you to-day about one of your very best friends,--one so altogether lovely, from first to last, that we can never exhaust her attractions.

Nature is, indeed, among the most loving and constant friends a girl can have, and not by any means the imaginary acquaintance so many suppose she is. She lives and breathes, and has a form and spirit. Are you looking about to see where she is? No need of that. Come right here, and sit down beside me under this great pine-tree. How strong and comfortable its back feels against yours! Do you see all those soft green points looking down on you while the tasselled branches gently sway? Just look at the deep blue patches of sky away up and up among the green arches. How cool and smooth and restful! how unending the color is in which the leaves lie! How hardy and brave the branches look! See the lines of beauty in them,--long, aspiring, slightly curving lines,--which meet and terminate in cathedral spires. What grace in the motion of every spray of greenness! what a healing odor in the breath of the tree! And, hark! a little breeze has touched it, and tuned its language into a plaintive song,--a sound like the surf washing upon a distant shore. Do you know why the pine is so sad a tree? Let me tell you her story. No; she will sing it herself, if you will listen to the nocturn: "Long, long ago I had my home on an island of the ocean, and my branches swayed and sang to the waves that kissed my feet with the fondness of a betrothed lover. The winds were envious of our sweet union, and blew away from me the germs of life. My seeds sprang up again, but on foreign soil; and the new trees, my offspring, are the same in form and color, but their souls are all sad from my recounted memories of departed joy." When the slightest breeze comes near, and ventures to softly touch the branches, a sound like sobbing follows; but when, with rougher grasp, the east wind approaches, a wailing like the utterances of a storm-tossed sea is heard. Listen! do you not hear it now? It is the imprisoned spirit of the pine, longing for the waves, moaning out a vain desire for the embrace of the sea.

How am I sure the tree is alive and friendly? Doesn't it bow to you when you pass, and curve and sweep before you? Doesn't it offer you rest and refreshment in its shade? Doesn't it entertain you by showing you beautiful pictures and forms, and doesn't it furnish you with music? See what an instructor it is! Away up there among the branches are lessons involving the very first principles of architecture, sculpture, and painting,--signs that show the laws of harmony and hint at morality itself. Its trunk and limbs look honest and courageous, firm and trusty, while all its lofty, tapering height points Godward.

It is your confidant; and the more you tell it, the more you will find to say. While it is very modest and retiring, requiring time to get acquainted with you, still, the more it talks to you, the more you will want to hear. The pine is your school-master, and you are the royal pupil,--Roger Ascham and Queen Elizabeth. It is no longer an ordinary tree, but something born with a spirit in it; and it has birthdays. Thoreau, the man who loved Nature so much that the birds and the fishes took care of him and were never afraid of their master, used to visit certain trees on certain days in the year. The pine has a birthday worth celebrating in December, the maple in October, and the birch in May. You think this is all fancy, and believe persons must be very imaginative to find such friends in Nature? Oh, no; along with fancy Nature tucks very real things into our thoughts about her. You only need an introduction to her, and you will see for yourselves. The most practical among you will find that even fancy is a most useful quality, because it leads men to think out great truths.

Some of the most remarkable ideas in literature, philosophy, science, and, religion have come from just this snug little acquaintance with Nature. Probably the most original poet in the last hundred years was Wordsworth. However much he lacked in some respects, he has done most towards shaping the minds of other poets, and towards advancing new and beautiful theories. His honest ideas, his simple truths, were told him by the field-flowers--the celandine and daisy and daffodil--as well as by the common trees and the common sky. I suppose most of the principles of natural philosophy, and of many of the sciences, must have been derived from an acquaintance with Nature in her ordinary aspects. Oh, do not think it necessary to behold Nature in her great stretches of sublimity in order to appreciate her. You will come to know her far more easily, and much more helpfully, in a little wood-side walk, or right here underneath these branches, than you will in Niagara Falls, or in looking at her in the great ocean. She comes down more to the level of your understanding here in this meadow. Comes down to your comprehension? Yes; I mean that, and yet I would not for a moment imply that in her most commonplace guise you can exhaust her beauty. Do you know what Mr. Ruskin says about such an apparently insignificant thing as a blade of grass? "Gather a single blade of grass, and examine for a minute, quietly, its narrow, sword-shaped strip of fluted green. Nothing it seems there, of notable goodness or beauty. A very little strength and a very little tallness, and a few delicate long lines meeting in a point.... And yet, think of it well, and judge whether of all the gorgeous flowers that beam in summer air, and of all strong and goodly trees, pleasant to the eyes and good for food,--stately palm and pine, strong ash and oak, scented citron, burdened vine,--there be any so deeply loved, by God so highly graced, as that narrow point of feeble green."

But *how* to get acquainted with Nature is the question. By observation,--by simply opening your eyes and seeing. If no one yet knows all about a blade of grass, surely no one has so far beheld all the beauty there is in a single sun-rise. You cannot see every thing at a glance. When you first let your eyes rest upon the horizon, you may see only a piece of sky in the east: not very remarkable, you think, except that here and there are things that look like streaks of red and yellow. Later, you find something unobserved before,--clouds shaped like islands and balanced in mid-air, or lying like rafts which float along the edge of the sky. Then the color seems to deepen, and to spread out in great bars of light which lift and remove the remnants of the night. They are floating barges,--gondolas richly decked with crimson and gold, and burning with jewels of light. A coolness seems to come in the air, an exhilaration in your feeling. Energy, enterprise, are inspired with the dawn. When the sun is really up in the heavens, you feel an expansion of spirits, and great light is within you. You, too, will make a path through the day, as the sun makes his path through the heavens. By and by you will be able to say with the bardic philosopher, "I see the spectacle of morning from the hill-top over against my house from daybreak to sunrise, with emotions which an angel might share ... I seem to partake its rapid transformations. The active enchantment reaches my dust, and I dilate and conspire with the morning wind ... Give me health and a day, and I will make the pomp of emperors ridiculous." And, at length, you will rise above the earthly, and exclaim with the psalmist, "Lift up your heads, O ye gates; and be ye lift up, ye everlasting doors; and the King of glory shall come in."

Observe the humblest flower that grows, and first you may notice only its color, or form, or fragrance. Look again, and some added beauty appears. Observe more closely, handle it, and you are made a little thoughtful, because, all unconsciously to yourself, it may be, the flower is doing something to your mind and heart and soul. Perhaps its velvety softness and its lowliness speak to you of humility and gentleness; or perhaps its fragrance breathes sweetness into your life and feeling,--only a little, to be sure, but that little means something. The spirit of the flower speaks to your spirit; and you wonder what relation it bears to you, and if you are not both connected with the spirit of God.

There is something more than sentiment in attributing character to flowers, something better than fancy in saying, "Pansies for thoughts." Growing things all mean real things; so do the stones in the stone-wall, and the gravel on the road, and the very breeze that blows in our faces,--all and each have a significance which does not at once meet the outward eye.

It would be very delightful, and certainly very useful, if, besides this friendliness in Nature, you could learn some of the special values of Nature, as shown by science. A botanist has fuller joy in flowers and ferns and grasses than a mere observer of them, and a geologist has more pleasure in rocks than he who remarks them for their beauty's sake. Still, this friendship and this general observation had to come before the scientific knowledge was possible. I have great sympathy for those who, while ignorant of technicalities, love objects for just simply the things themselves.

When you begin to get acquainted with the externals of Nature, then, of course, you will ask how they are made; and the lessons of science will attract you. Looking at the smoothness of the rounded stones, you will be led to examine their ancient homes beneath the waves; noticing the long straight lines on the rocks, you will wander back to the period when ice covered the land, and the earth was wrapped in chaotic gloom. Observe, only observe! and curiosity will press for you the very secrets out of the woods, the streams, the skies. Look around you! There is such an infinite number of objects to consider right about your own porch-door,--the lichens on the door-stone, the apple-tree shading the path, the striped pebble that you kick aside, the plant pressing up between the boards, the dew shimmering on the weed. Investigate all your surroundings, especially the small, neglected places, and try to have an opinion about what you observe. A busy man, a merchant, noticed, some time ago, a thistle growing by the wayside. He was journeying in the steam-cars at the time; and, although the next stopping-place was somewhat far, he walked back to find the strange flower. The prize he gained was a rare plant, a beautiful thistle of which he had only heard before.

Oh, Nature is so modest! But once set her talking, she will forget your presence, and babble like the brook. How much she has told the poets, and the men of science! How much she will tell you, too, if you but heed her!

Ah, girls, what slight attention we have, in reality, shown to Nature! We treat her more like a servant than a friend and companion. The desire for excitement has turned our minds to vainer subjects. The struggles which our elders have made for money and position have deprived them of chances for regarding natural objects. However deplorable this may be, it is a still more lamentable fact, that you, dear girls, give so little heed to Nature,--you who have time and to spare. It lies with you to cultivate this love for the natural world, that future generations may be more mindful of it.

When we refuse the gladness that Nature offers us, we dismiss a large share of the happiness God intended for us. I ought to be a little more lenient in my criticism on the lack of appreciating Nature, perhaps; for not a few of us may find lingering in our minds some autumnal glory which lights up our memories with colors of crimson and gold. We should remember, however, that not only the glow of autumn and the flush of summer are beautiful, but that every season, every climate, every aspect in the shifting panorama of Nature, has a beauty as real. Our own region, be it arid with parching suns, or wet with frequent rains; be it always winter there, or always summer, is full of beauty. There is sunset on the desert, moonrise on mid-ocean, gorgeous coloring and crowding life in the tropics, dazzling starlight over ice-bound lands. Neither is one day so much better than another for beholding Nature. Yesterday we let the mild sunshine redden the blood beneath the skin; to-day we are drawn from our study of the perfect harmony of grays in the clouds and trees to watch, within the house, the bright light which gleams from the coals,--Nature brought up out of the earth.

Regard even one day of our worst weather, as we say,--worst for our health or convenience we must always mean. Think of a bleak and sleety March day. As the storm whirls against the house with strong blasts of rain and snow, our excitement increases by watching the swaying trees, and by listening to the shaking windows, while the lawless winds howl and rage around the corner. When the winds settle from boisterousness into low complaints, and now and then fall into quiet utterances, musical murmurings, the rain pauses, the sky softens, and our minds grow calm and gentle. But when, again, the clouds gather darkness, and make strength for a new onslaught, we become sober with fear and doubt. Tell me, if, as we view these changes, and hear these stirring or weird sounds, we do not indeed behold battle scenes, and listen to music from which even Wagner might have learned.

But the storm is the exceptional aspect, and we ought to care more for ordinary views. Winter is common enough, but it has its perfections. Its colors, though less gorgeous than those of autumn, are the most restful and quiet in their tone and feeling. Those grays and browns, huddling together in silent lines side by side, are full of peaceful beauty as they rest upon the white snow or up against uncertain skies. I like a gray atmosphere relieved by silver birches, just enough sombreness set off by cheerfulness. It is wisdom and patience ornamented with gray locks.

Spring, early spring, in New England, we call more disagreeable than winter. Ah, but it is the budding time! When you meet spring, before the trees come out in full dress, when all that fluttering, fluffy greenness, and that crimson flowering etch, with innumerable branchlets, the embroidery of Nature against the sky, you meet, even though the east sea winds blow, a season incomparable.

An opportunity for getting acquainted with Nature is never wanting. If men should cut down all the forest trees, as they now threaten, they could not "cut the clouds out of the sky," as Thoreau affirms. A roof light in a garret, even, gives the eye visions dazzlingly beautiful over beyond all the chimney pots, if the eye only looks. We would go far to see on canvas the lake, the river, the wood that borders our heritage; and yet we rarely heed their living charms that daily offer us new pleasures. We cross the ocean to visit great churches, and we throng to hear an organ played by a master musician; while in yonder forest we may enter a cathedral, loftier and grander far than art can form, through whose densely branching arches and solemn aisles sweeps the music of the winds from the organ pipes of the pines.

Nature, in most of her aspects, will give us small chance for censuring her scant attractions. A field of grass and flowers, sunshine and chirping birds, the clinging, changing foliage, or the shimmer of snow and ice, the light of moon and stars, are in some of her commonest pictures. We are simply to give heed. As Carlyle suggests, it is not because we have such superior levity that we pay no attention to Nature. By not thinking, we simply cease to wonder, that is all.

Oh, get acquainted with Nature, my girls, and see how lovely the world will become! Do you know that beautiful sketch by Charles Kingsley called "My Winter Garden"? Read it, and see how he gets the world out of a small space,--how he becomes rich. You know no man can buy a landscape,--it belongs to all. We are, every one, rich in summer skies, in fair forests, in great tracts of meadow verdure. See how Kingsley grows contented,--how he becomes wise. "Have you eyes to see? Then lie down on the grass, and look near enough to see something more of what is to be seen; and you will find tropic jungles in every square foot of turf; mountain cliffs and debacles at the mouth of every rabbit burrow; dark strids, tremendous cataracts, 'deep glooms and sudden glories' in every foot-broad rill which wanders through the turf.... Nature, as every one will tell you who has seen dissected an insect under the microscope, is as grand and graceful in her smallest as in her largest forms."

We are told there is something most practical in physiology. One of its first requirements is proper exercise for the body. Now, no exercise combines so many advantages as walking: by no other means can we come so easily to an acquaintance with Nature. Never ride in the country, or anywhere within Nature's dearest precincts, when you can as well go on foot. You cannot see things flying by you. Do not adopt the custom of most pedestrians, that of getting over the ground as rapidly as possible. Take daily walks, no matter what the weather is; but do not go too far. Irregularity in this exercise is harmful. It is far better to walk two miles daily than ten miles at one time, and fifteen a week hence. Go to see something on your walks, if you discover nothing more than a great hole in the ground; and come home with some thought about what you have seen. I found out a great truth, one day last spring, of which I was wholly ignorant before,--that a rose is sweeter in the morning than in the noonday. Many a lesson in that; some practical knowledge too.

In a delightful way, the hermit of Walden tells us how to take walks, how to truly saunter. He says that the word saunterer was derived from those persons who, during the Middle Ages, went on crusades to the Holy Land. When one of them, as he journeyed towards the East, appeared among the children, they would exclaim, "'There goes a Sainte Terrer!'--a Holy Lander"--which, you can see, came to be called "Saunterer." Thoreau says that every one who walks as he should, with his eyes and his heart open, is bound to a Holy Land. "Every walk is a sort of crusade, preached by some Peter the Hermit in us, to go forth and reconquer this Holy Land from the hands of the Infidels." Is not that a beautiful thought?

Walk with freedom of the chest and limbs, carrying nothing in the hands to prevent the play of any muscles. Breathe through the nose rather than through the mouth. I suppose the most of the girls can walk in an ordinary street dress; but I would suggest, if a girl is to go far, that she wear a full, short skirt, of not very heavy weight, a loose flannel blouse, and stout shoes. This costume can be arranged so that it will not in the least shock her townspeople. It is always safest, and usually most agreeable, to walk accompanied by one or more friends who are bound on the same quest. Begin your walk as you are to continue it: at an even, easy pace, or with such steps as you naturally take when the first signs of weariness appear. Use as much of your body as you can. Welcome the increased circulation of the blood, and the glow of the skin; but be very careful to retard these when you are nearing the end of your saunter, or are about to rest for a while. Remember the danger of standing or sitting quietly when in a perspiration.

It is profitable to rest early in a walk, and to break it by frequently sitting down for a few moments at a time. Do not walk too rapidly. Remember you are not to care who gets to the top of the mountain first. It should be your aim to see things on the way up, as well as from the summit. If one often turns to get views from behind, the ascent gradually prepares one's mind for the climacteric vision from the top. You may boast that you have walked a given number of miles, but count yourself still prouder because you have seen what that number of miles held for you along the way.

Be careful of your steps, yet be bold and confident, that you may leap the stream or scale the rock. If you stop to reflect, the stream will grow wider, and the rock steeper and smoother. A stick helps many in climbing, but I believe the skilled pedestrian climbs unaided. Do **not** jump, girls. Creep, slide, crawl; but never shock your system with a jump of few or many feet in height.

The dangers of walking arise from too great an ambition to go a long distance, from striving to out-walk somebody, from walking too rapidly and irregularly, and from allowing the mind to become so exhilarated as not to be sensible of the fatigues of the body. Stop when you are tired. Remember that, in a walk of ten miles, the last five are longer than the first five; then reserve that second half for the next day.

Form observation clubs, mountain clubs, pedestrian clubs,--any worthy association which will take you out of doors, and teach you about the region in which you live. Be earnest about it, as about a solemn, necessary work. Take your English cousins for examples. I think it was Sara Coleridge who, in her old age, complained because she could no longer walk more than fifteen miles a day. In that delightful essay, written by Charles Lamb, on "Old China," Bridget Elia sighs because she and her companion have become so rich they cannot walk their thirty miles, as they had so often done, on a holiday.

In England or in Switzerland, one meets whole flocks of English girls out on a walk of a week's duration. Think of the sport in such a tramp,--the hilarity on the way! the lunches gathered by hap-hazard from country bake-shops and groceries, and eaten in any retired nook that offers by the roadside! Think of the appetite for commonest food, and of the amusing difficulties which come from lack of knives and forks! On such a walk, how easy to pick one's self up after lunch, throw the dinner-table away, and trot on to the next village. As a girl passes from town to town, how eager she is to note their characteristics, to look at the people curiously, and to pry into their shop-windows. How much she learns about Nature! Is the sky so blue at home? Are the wild flowers so abundant? Is the grass so soft and green? Oh, girls! try to make yourselves at home with Nature, and walk out among her attractions. In all your observations of Nature do not forget her living personality, her power to love you, to comfort you, and to develop you. Feel that you have a friend with you even when you seem to go solitary. Remember that, in learning to know Nature, you are learning to know yourselves. From your friends and your books, ask all about what you see. Be favored with every grand spectacle in Nature, but be never wearied with her commonplace aspects. Do not think of yourselves so much as living in rooms and houses, but as living in *the* house, the palace of the earth and sky, whose every gallery, corridor and hall, is carpeted with Nature's tapestries of unfading color and deep softness; whose walls are hung with glowing sunsets; and through whose green roof, here and there, "a pane of blue sky" appears.

III.
HOW TO MAKE THE MOST OF WORK.

When God made heaven and earth, and all things beautiful for the enjoyment of his children, He added His last, best blessing,--the gift of work. Sweeter than the fruits of Eden, more grateful than the fragrance that breathed from the flowers of Paradise, and grander than all the starry hosts of heaven, was this most precious favor. By it the world is delivered of its hidden riches, and the mind of man developed into its broadest capabilities. Yes, dear girls, there is a blessedness in work that transcends every joy you have. You know it; but the question comes, How to make the most of the gift?

What a dull old world this would be if we spent all our days on hotel verandas at summer resorts! Absolutely unbearable! We should all die of ease. It is as necessary for us all to work as it is to breathe. Nothing exists in the natural world without its special office or duty; and surely, in the world of man, no one can live without occupation. Lack of sufficiently worthy work is one of the crying evils of our day, among both boys and girls. Every thing is done to make labor less, or to turn it completely into pleasure,--to shirk it, or to scorn it. The sewing-machine has made the good sewer a phenomenon. Our grandmothers used to rip their dresses and linings with sharp scissors: a good jump from a carriage will send us right out of a modern costume. Teachers learn the lessons now, and the pupils take notes and cram once in a while. Text-books have gone out of fashion. The next generation will not see any antique furniture: it will all lie in a hopelessly unglued state, separated into its elements. There will not be any china tea-sets,--all broken in the last dish-washing. There may be a few books in loose bindings and faded covers, and a few works of art in frames that furnace-heat has set sadly awry. There will be a plenty of fine machines.

Mr. Froude tells us, "When the magnificent Earl of Essex was sent to Cambridge, in Elizabeth's time, his guardian provided him with a deal table covered with green baize, a truckle-bed, half a dozen chairs, and a wash hand-basin. The cost of all was five pounds." Harvard boys have somewhat enlarged that invoice of housekeeping goods. What do you think about the furnishings of college girls?

Welcome improvement. Yes, indeed! Be glad of clothes-wringers, dish- washers, carpet-sweepers, Quincy methods, Meisterschaft systems, and all else that will economize labor and time, or make more attractive the special work you have to do; but never forget that no machine can be invented which will make housekeeping a sport, and thorough, hard work of any kind unnecessary. And remember, too, there is no royal road to learning, as the Alexandrian philosopher said. Kings and queens must walk over the same rough road which we tread when they go up to the temple of knowledge. Cloth of gold cannot smooth the way, nor elegant editions make knowledge more subservient.

Girls, what do you think about shirking work? One of the chief differences between happy girls and moody ones consists in the amount of work they do, or leave undone. The despair which settles over many a girl's days, the indifference, comes from no longer being compelled to do certain tasks. "Get work, get work: be sure 'tis better than what you work to get." Do not delay the task that must be done. Procrastination is worse than the thief of time: it is the robber of our own character, our own growth and happiness. We need to work continually to be strong, mentally, physically, or spiritually, even; and the longer we put off exercise, the less competent we are. I cannot believe that a lazy person is a real Christian. Who labors, prays. I know so many girls who delay writing essays, hoping that slight sickness, or some unforeseen event, may ward off the trouble of thinking for an hour; then, when the time of necessity comes, and no deliverance from the hands of tyrannical teachers, a series of nervous attacks ensue, because of overtaxed minds (?); and the doctors order those poor girls out of the presence of such cruel task-masters. Medical science and educational science always do conflict; but eleven-o'clock suppers, social circles, tri-weekly gad-abouts, and over-anxious parents, who yearn for a good match for their daughters, disarrange the brains and stomachs of girls oftener than any undue desire to excel in study. The average student is never killed by the average school or the average school-teacher. But shirking work of any kind, delaying it, or contriving to make it less, will bring about a certain irregularity, and certain spasmodic efforts that are utterly ruinous.

The cramming system, in schools, or homes, or trades, is deplorable. You cannot put a whole geometry into your brain three days before examination, without its bulging and breaking through the cranium in less than a month's time. You cannot sweep and bake and wash Saturday morning, without the pies burning, the clothes tearing, and the dust flying. You cannot do all your book-keeping in just the hour before the evening train starts: some one's account will be incorrect. Regularity achieves what intensity never can. It is not the amount of work that hurts, so much as spasmodic attempts to work. Girls are not as strong as formerly. Irregular work, fast work, fast living, are largely at fault. Girls scorn work: it is too humble, or too little appreciated. Now, the fact is, girls, there is highest worth and dignity in precisely those kinds of labor that seem the lowliest and count for the least. Kinds of work differ, not so much in worth as in the use they make of our faculties to do to our utmost what lies before us. The monotony of housekeeping, or the daily repetition of work immediately to be undone, is, after all, the most essential labor. Without it, especially in America, the home would be destroyed. "If a woman is not fit to manage the internal matters of a house, she is fit for nothing, and should never be put in a house or over a house, any way. Good housekeeping lies at the root of all the real ease and satisfaction in existence."[2]

It is an offence to women everywhere that in summing up women's work, the census will carefully enumerate those employed in professions,-- doctors, lawyers, ministers, teachers, authors,--those who work in factories and clothing establishments; those who are accountants, manufacturers, servants, farmer's, and fishwomen, even; but contains not one word about the home-keepers. Are they not in any profession? Have they no valuable calling? Enrolled, would not they swell the number of workers by several hundreds of thousands in Massachusetts alone? If the census slights home-keepers, however, the girls slight home-keeping even more. Very few girls are to step aside from the commonplace, as we carelessly term it; but more depends, in this world, on the ordinary than the extraordinary. The work of the humblest is as essential to the labor of the highest as is the work of the highest to the labor of the lowliest. Michael Angelo could plan a St. Peter's; but the men who

---

2 Harriet Prescott Spofford.

climbed up with wood and stone--"the hewers of wood and the drawers of water"--were necessary to its construction. Genius is a slave to labor. Says Smiles, in his work on "Thrift," "Genius is but a capability of laboring intensely"; making, you see, even talent itself, and its highest expression, an outgrowth of work.

No simplest task we do but is essential to somebody. Slight it, shirk it, scorn it, and somebody suffers. Leave the parlor undusted, and callers are sure to come. Wear a stocking with a hole in it, you will find it necessary to take your boot off before night. There is the greatest need among girls of a more entire consecration to certain humble, homely, housewifely duties. The wearing torment of discontent with unassuming work arises not from lack of ambition, but from scorn of what one has to do. I sometimes think this reaching out after the unattainable is worse for a girl than passive indifference to what she might acquire. A large part of the success a person achieves is dependent upon her thinking her calling the very best in the world. It is not the work which dignifies you: it is you who dignify the work.

The girl who wins honor in medicine, in literature, in music, in engineering, in astronomy, in laundry-work, in cookery, in needle-work, ennobles literature, or music, or science, or housekeeping. What worthy pursuit can you not, by excellence, raise into honor and esteem? Matilda of Normandy embroidered, in the quiet of her castle, stitch by stitch, and day after day, the battle of Hastings, at which the Conqueror won. When that great mingling of Normans and Saxons proved to be the important and the last step in the making of England, men looked back to the battle which decided the Norman Conquest, and, lacking needed information from chronicles, turned to the work of Matilda. There, on the Bayeux tapestry, was wrought the battle scene they required,--a piece of woman's work. It was a peasant girl, you know, who brought victory to France in the Hundred Years' War between that country and England.

Girls and boys have too slight an appreciation of manual labor. In most ways, work with the hands is more necessary than mental labor. God made man work in a garden before he gave him power to write books or keep accounts. Fine white hands are very pretty when they belong to a lady; but sunburnt, muscular ones are beautiful in the vineyard.

May I warn you not to despise the small amount of work you can accomplish, as compared with what others are able to do? Let me remind you, too, it is not what we get in money, buildings, knowledge, reputation, influence, by means of work, so much as what labor does for ourselves, our characters. Carlyle expressed the idea in a very short sentence, "Not what I have, but what I do, is my kingdom."

Even if our work is spoilt as we near its completion, and, instead of gain, failure awaits us, we have still been winners in ourselves, because we have acquired habits of industry, have made our powers of perseverance stronger, and have developed physical or mental strength as well. Work is never lost. When Carlyle sat down to write his "French Revolution" the second time,--a careless servant having burnt his manuscript,--he was a nobler man than when he wrote out the first issue. When Walter Scott failed, and Abbotsford was encumbered with a large debt, when his dream of restoring a kind of baronial life was all shattered, he did a grander work than in the building of that magnificent estate; for he strove with all the powers of his mind to earn the money which should repay his creditors. Though he died in the struggle, it was not fought in vain.

IV.
WHAT CAN I DO?

B ut what can I do?" you ask. Oh, I hear that so many, many times, and I feel the deepest sympathy for the girl who asks it. Usually, when the question is put, there is no marked ability in the asker,--I mean, no special power to do a particular work. I have hardly the right to say this, however, since we are all endowed in some way, and each girl must have a work in which she can do better than any other. Perhaps, girls, you belong to the great middle class,--the people who have no large fortunes, no particular influence; and, maybe, you think if you only had a rich relative, or some acquaintance, who stood in authority, you might do a good work, or, at least, earn a livelihood. Do you remember that this very class of people have been the greatest reformers, thinkers, workers, rulers, everywhere? The United States owes its existence to people who had to depend upon themselves.

But let us see about this question, what to do. In the first place, if a girl has a decided inclination towards this or that honorable calling, she should foster every opportunity for pursuing it. If she can do a nurse's work better than a teacher's, and if no home ties of an imperative nature restrain her, she ought to become a nurse. A large field for the special work of nursing has been opened during late years. In all our prominent hospitals we find training-schools for nurses. The girl who feels she is fairly strong, and who has a good amount of physical courage, does a brave deed when she goes into the hospital to become a nurse. When she graduates, fitted to render service to the sick, and willing to devote her life to them, she is a noble acquisition to the world's helpers.

If a girl can do most and best as a physician or surgeon, she ought to be always the doctor. We no longer question the right or ability of women to practise medicine. The time will come when women will be as numerous in the medical profession as men. A girl ought to be very sure of a few things, however, before she studies medicine with a view to practising. There are peculiar hardships in a doctor's life, requiring physical strength, continuous toil, strong nerves, decision, reticence, and indifference to unjust criticism. With natures more susceptible than young men possess, be sure, girls, that you are equal to the burdens that weigh so heavily on the shoulders of the boys.

If a girl can cook better than she can do other work, the kitchen ought to claim her. Schools of cookery have made of cooking an art to be industriously followed where success is desired. Superintendents of cooking are usually reliable persons, and command good salaries. In a smaller way, many a girl in town or country can turn her knowledge of cooking to advantage, by selling her cake, or jelly, or pickles, for a snug little sum. There is a call for such prepared food not only in the industrial rooms of cities, but in country shops as well. We buy Miss M.'s orange cake, and Miss F.'s spiced pickles; for the one makes her cake, and the other her pickles, better, much better, than others do. The world always wants the best in small as well as in great things, and will pay for it.

Should a girl enjoy the cultivation of plants, she would be able to give much pleasure to her friends by caring for a private conservatory or window-garden. In this way she could learn much about plants, and become a successful florist. Then, if there were reasons why she should earn a living, with a small capital she could gradually work into the cultivation of flowers to such an extent as to make them very serviceable money-makers.

Sometimes girls have a fondness for fowls, and like to accumulate pin- money from the eggs hens lay. Why should they not give much time to the care of poultry? try for fine breeds, and for eggs that bring the highest prices?

A good deal has been written recently in relation to the cultivation of the silk-worm as a means of creating an occupation for girls and women, and as a method of forwarding American industries. The results already attained in this work are valuable and highly promising. Very earnest women are encouraging its progress, and will gladly supply any needed information in regard to it. Girls, you will come to see that women of large hearts and generous souls are deeply interested in your welfare. I hope every city has such noble examples of this kind of women as Boston presents. If you wish to know more about silk culture, please refer to Miss Marian McBride of the "Boston Post."

I have cited sufficient examples to urge that, if desire turns a girl to this or that occupation, she ought to seek it and follow it, provided, always, her judgment is as clear as her wish is ardent. Remembering that a lady is such of herself, whether in a drawing-room or an attic, behind the counter or in the school-room, a girl will be of noble worth, and will become one place as well as another. I do believe in choice of work; but I believe even more strongly in a girl's preserving the "eternally womanly," whatever she does, and wherever she is.

In most cases, a woman's work and place are in her own home. "Wherever a true wife comes, home is always round her. The stars only may be over her head, the glow-worm in the night-cold grass may be the only fire at her foot; but home is yet wherever she is: and for a noble woman it stretches far round her, better than ceiled with cedar, or painted with vermilion, shedding its quiet light far, for those who else were homeless."[3]

As a girl is bound to do what she honestly feels she can do best, she should never question how her work may seem to another, if it does not absolutely injure another. I should not ask is this man's work or woman's work; but, rather, is it my work? But, in whatever I attempted, I should repeatedly say to myself, Am I keeping my womanhood strong and real, as God intended it? am I working womanly? In many cases, much more good might be accomplished by girls and women, if, instead of so much talk about lacking privileges, they took the places they could fill. Sister Dora never questioned whether she ought to bind up the wounds of her crushed workmen: she laid them on the beds of her hospital, and calmly healed them. Caroline Herschel did not stop to ask whether her telescope were privileged to find new stars, but swept it across the heavens, and was the first discoverer of at least five comets. A great obstacle in the way of advancement to girls comes from the coarse mannerism of certain women who have worked in given directions. Why is it that, when a woman begins to do the work a man has been accustomed to perform, she cultivates a man's ways? It is not the work which does it. Would that there might be less of this unwomanliness! Because a woman is a doctor, why need she use slang or profanity? Because she holds certain great, liberal truths in regard to woman,

3　Ruskin.

why must she wear a stiff derby, swagger, and strike attitudes? These expressions, extremes in dress, conspicuous actions, deceive many, and turn the world bitterly against what it ought to receive. Such peculiarities are wholly unnecessary. Some of the loveliest women who walk the earth are found among doctors, among professors, among book-makers, among farmers, even.

You think there is less chance for girls to work than for boys? Yes, there is; but, on an examination of statistics, I find that in all positions--professions, clerkships, manufactures, trades, industries-- where you find men working, you will find women also, though in smaller numbers usually. Examine the reports of census takers, and you will find my statement true. In Mr. Wright's valuable pamphlet on "The Working Girls of Boston," you will be surprised to find so great a variety of employments as he there enumerates. There are recorded merchants, machinists, carpenters, plumbers, cabinet-makers, and tanners, even.

Why is it so many of you girls try teaching? Is it because that seems a genteel way to get a living, and does not seem so hard as other callings? In 1880 there were 8,562 women engaged in teaching in Massachusetts. Of these, a fourth would probably have done a better work in some other way. Teaching is a noble profession: it has great chances for self-culture and for helpfulness to others. In no profession can one do more good, if one tries with all one's heart. It is one of the highest callings even for this reason: a teacher utterly unable to see any results of her labor, in black and white, at the end of her pupil's course, as the book-maker may see in the number of printed pages, is willing to trust that, because she has done what she could, good will come to her pupil. A carpenter may see his house completed; but the building of mind, of character, of manhood and womanhood, the teacher never may see finished. It passes on into the hands of the great Teacher of all. Although teaching is a very responsible work, yet does one seldom reach fame in it. The truth is, fame does not stand for so much work done, but for so much worldly opinion gained. Do not enter this work of teaching to misunderstand or slight it, but to be proud of it, and to ennoble it.

You feel the necessity of earning money, and so must take whatever work you can get? Alas! I know you do, many of you, dear girls. But do not think this so very unfortunate. Unless your very life is being worn out; unless your wages are ground down to a pittance, and your work is wholly disagreeable, be thankful. You are as well off as the girls who are languishing with dissipation and **ennui**. The average girl has the average amount of hardship and blessing in her life. I know there are many girls who cannot be found among the average.

If there is no wish on a girl's part to follow a special work, if she has no marked ability, let her ask the advice of friends; but, more than that, let her seek, through her own personal efforts, some honest work. Pluck, not luck; the Yankee, not the aristocrat, earn a living. For a girl of average ability I think a mingling of manual and mental labor preferable to purely manual or strictly mental work. There are many authors, journalists, accountants, etc., who have achieved striking success; but ordinarily this success has sprung from certain brilliant or profound mental attributes. Hand labor that requires no thought does not exercise our best faculties. I cannot specify just here what occupations an average girl may undertake. I gladly refer to certain books which contain statistics of work and its profits, or which suggest occupations: "The Working Girls of Boston," by Carroll D. Wright; "Think and Act, Men and Women, Work and Wages," by Virginia Penney; "What Girls Can Do," by Phillis Brown.

My poor girls, who work so hard, so very hard, who seem daily to narrow all enjoyment, and to give your very existence to factories and looms, to dry-goods counters and ready-made clothing stores, who put your eyes out earning twenty-five cents a day, and sometimes put your souls out trying to keep breath in your bodies one short year more,--what shall I say to you? I cannot find the words to tell you what I would say. Your experience shall not be embittered by being told what to do and what not to do. Bear your work as well as you can, try to find something really good about it, do not slight it. Remember you make the world noble; and, if you have an absorbing desire to work in some other way, watch every little loop-hole of opportunity, and see if you cannot make it large enough to jump through to a wider field. Let us all avoid fickleness, however,--the doing a little of this and of that: it is poor economy. To grow up to a work, to master it, we must first be slaves to it. Girls, everywhere, make progress slowly,--**grow** in efficiency, and do not shoot up into it.

Now, I want to talk a little to the girls who have leisure,--so much of it, sometimes, that it all turns crazy on their hands, and expends itself in the last most fashionable excitement. Girls too often do things just because other girls are doing them, never for a moment considering fitness or ability; consequently they look back upon half- accomplished bits of work--this or that insanity in worsted, cardboard, wood-carving, modelling, or darning--very much as they would upon the broken fragments of an upset dinner-table. Away up in that convenient attic lie the desecrated splendors of the past, scattered in confusion by charitable mice,--blue and crimson wax-flowers melt underneath the eaves, all destitute of petals that would not fit on; patchwork quilts and cushions, in silk and satin distractions, just fall short of harmony in the arrangement of their squares and colors; vivid buttercups and daisies mingle with bulky cat-o'-nine-tails,--all on canvas covered with paint; blacking-jugs adorned with pictures, embossed and otherwise; moth-eaten Kensington, partly outlined in conventional lilies and conventional stitches; forlorn-looking cats and dogs on half-made rugs and slippers,--all, all are there to point out certain very unpleasant morals, referring chiefly to inability and lack of perseverance.

Understand, to excel in worsted, in painting, in any of the arts which afford so much pleasure, even in amateur work, is highly commendable. Perhaps to dip into these occupations to pass time might be considered better than laziness. But to do them simply because others are following them is wholly unwarrantable. I do not believe in crazes,--do you? What is worth doing is worth pursuing.

Intense interest may be necessary to success; but extremes make us very abrupt, inconsistent, and fickle in our occupations. Test the quality of your last attempt to make a tree on canvas before you buy a full set of colors, and before you put out your sign as an artist. Much study, hard work, aptitude, are required by art;--and the phenomenal ***debut*** of a fully fledged artist "after ten lessons" ("the whole art taught in six weeks") will never be witnessed. I should say, before passing further, that even a slight acquaintance with the decorative arts as practised at present appears to be quite improving to one's taste, and cultivating to the perceptions.

Music--singing, playing--is a great accomplishment. Would that every girl might know its precious helps,--its sources of amusement and culture, and the divine mysteries of its art. But unless you can express the musician's thought, and interpret harmonies by harmony, never be afraid to say, "I cannot play."

If the crazes which now threaten to capture society, and to seriously affect the speech, work, dress, and accomplishments of young ladies, continue at their present rate, I think there will be a grand chance for escape from them. It will suddenly become the fashion to be tranquil, plain of speech, real and thorough in every work. Now we strive our utmost to prevent monotony, and promote variety. The dressmaker's trade we learn in 1885 will not be of much use in 1886. Last winter we learned how to cook; and this, we are studying how to cure by mental processes. Next year we shall go to the gymnasium and tighten up our muscles. After that, we may open sewing-schools; and, perhaps, later, turn our attention to literature classes.

There are so many things a girl can do, even when society claims her,-- more than ever, I should say! Make work, if you cannot get it, girls. Encourage poor girls by joining the industrial unions instituted in their behalf. Go into the hospitals, old ladies' homes, charity bureaus, flower missions. Join a Chautauqua club, or one of the societies for the encouragement of studies at home. That one founded in Boston for home studies, and which now numbers many hundreds, affords excellent instruction, particularly in literature and history. This educational society has done a wonderful amount of good through correspondence, books loaned, criticisms, examinations. Attend the numerous lectures, exhibits, etc., which are provided free of expense in all large cities.

Do not be afraid of useful fancy work. One can rest delightfully while making a row on an afghan, or knitting on a bed slipper. I always pity a boy who never seems to have any way of occupying himself while he rests. He whistles, puffs a cigarette, perhaps, or whittles away the window-seat. Girls have no need of being lazy while they rest. They certainly will not sit in lawless indifference if they know the blueness of discontent. Cheerful people are workers; and, when they find any tendency to go "mooning" over their tasks, they shake themselves into broad daylight.

I have suggested but a few of the things girls can do with greatest profit to themselves and to others. Form reading associations, hygiene societies, relief clubs, emergency clubs, horticultural unions, charity bureaus, science clubs, painting clubs. Why are they not just as entertaining as progressive euchre clubs? You know a girl never does as well when no incentive is placed before her; so I have hinted at the value of organization for general improvement, for work, and for larger usefulness in every sense. The modern sewing-circle, the missionary associations, even the temperance organizations in churches, have frequently been most efficient means of holding churches together. Clubs for boys are not so strongly recommended as for girls, because these associations for young men come to be their dependence for entertainment, and consume the hours which ought to be spent at home, or in the society of both girls and boys. Club-life in England, particularly London, has taken the place of home-life. Now, the girls need have no fear from their associations, because they are formed principally to forward the interests of home.

Work, then, girls! Work for pleasure, work for profit! Work for the health of your bodies, and the health of your souls! "You will find that the mere resolve not to be useless, and the honest desire to help other people, will, in the quickest and most delicate ways, improve yourselves." "When men are rightly occupied their amusement grows out of their work, as the color petals out of a fruitful flower; when they are faithfully helpful and compassionate, all their emotions become steady, deep, perpetual, and vivifying to the soul as the natural pulse to the body."[4]

But whatever your work is, girls, do not be in too much of a hurry for great results. If there is any thing in old countries that strongly impresses the American mind, it is, probably, the great amount of labor, the infinite patience, and the centuries of time, that were necessary to construct their public edifices. We cannot understand such waits, such slow progress. On the contrary, the fact that most impresses the mind of a foreigner in our own streets is the hurry, impatience, rush and scramble of American life. The people walk along the narrow streets of Boston with such hurried steps, such deeply-seamed faces, such infinite anxieties, as if they were about to adjust the foundations of the earth, and had about two minutes to spare before applying the lever. Go slowly, girls, and your work will last the longer.

Do not expect to complete your line of reading or study in one winter. Do not await a large salary for the first year's work. Do not hope to more than initiate a charitable society in one autumn. Then try to remember the necessity of concentrating forces, and of bringing your heaviest action to bear on one point: too many undertakings dissipate strength and prostrate work. There is a great deal of poor work done now; and it is said to have been somewhat mediocre so far through the nineteenth century, because time enough has not been taken to do thorough work. The strong desire is to get to the end of toil. We have hardly time to think what to get for dinner or what to wear; but we get something to eat when we are hungry,

4 Ruskin

and go out into the cold wearing a spring jacket.

Now, one good, strong word more for work. We are born to enjoy and use it; civilization depends upon it, our womanhood is strengthened by it, our talents increased, our chances of happiness multiplied, and our service in every department of life is made worthier by the doing with our might just what lies before us.

V.
WHAT TO STUDY.

How much girls think they will do when they get out of school! How many books they think they will read!--histories of Greece and of Rome, Grote and Curtius, of Plutarch and Gibbon; histories of France, Germany, and England, Guizot, Ranke, Green and Freeman; biographies of Caesar, Leo, Lorenzo, Frederick, Elizabeth, and Napoleon! How they will feed on the literature of modern nations, from Chaucer through Tennyson; from Luther through Goethe; from Rabelais through Victor Hugo; from Bryant and Irving through Hawthorne and Longfellow! How much they will translate from Homer and Virgil and Tacitus; from Schiller, Racine, Fenelon, and Moliere! How much philosophy they will read from Darwin, Spencer, Huxley! How they will trace the stars in the heavens, and the marks of God's fingers on the rocks and sands! How they will separate into their parts water and air, plants and animals! How they will haunt the libraries, museums, laboratories, and lecture-rooms!--all when they get out of school.

Oh, my dear girls, you will not do any of these things unless you have much leisure, and an eager thirst for knowledge. Some new fascination-- society and pleasures--or special duties and pressing occupations will drive the fervid desires of your school-days quite from your hearts, or make it impossible for you to gratify them. At any rate, in attempting to pursue all these studies, you will find that neither the ordinary length of life, nor the average brain, will be sufficient for the work. Your lists of books, like your lists of intentions, will serve only to fill the waste-paper baskets.

But now let us see what you can do, girls, if you will. Almost every one of you spends a few hours a week in reading, and some of you pour away "oceans of time" over fashionable fiction. Why not give just two or three little hours to study,--study so pleasant and so arranged that you may call it reading, or recreating, or getting acquainted with "the best of all good company"? After a while you will find these hours precious and necessary. They will give you rest, and a greater number of useful and pleasant subjects to think about; they will afford you broader and readier information; and they will deepen within you an interest in the highest and most helpful things this life affords.

What we get in the average school is largely rudimentary knowledge, the object of which is to create a love for more knowledge, to bend our inclinations towards what is true and right, to prepare our minds for larger duties,--in a word, to fit us for a noble womanhood and a useful citizenship.

Now, suppose you feel more kindly towards natural science than you do towards mathematics; or suppose you have more fondness for language than for philosophy: well, just at this period, since you are really out of school, you ought to spend a few spare hours on the object of your favor. You should branch off from the trunk of knowledge, and flourish mainly in one direction, when you will find it will take all the time you can give to grow into any size, and blossom into one kind of fruitage.

There are so many things to learn in any department of knowledge, and the amount increases so rapidly, year by year, that, after a certain measure of general information has been acquired in the schools, it is almost necessary to make rigid choice of what we shall study, or of what we shall read. This may be narrowing, and even superficial, in one sense, since it confines our information within one channel, and prevents it from mingling with the ebb and flow of broader human interests. It may make us too regardless of any pursuit aside from our own, and bring us to the condition which many a foreigner finds himself in,--that of holding a complete knowledge about his own trade, but utter ignorance of every other. But I think not. If we are really intelligent, and comprehend the difficulties of the department of knowledge we are working in, I believe we have respect for the department another fills, though we know nothing of it. Of course, we are always to consider that the study we have chosen is best for us, and, therefore, to be lovingly and jealously followed. I think the method of choosing special studies is the only way of acquiring thorough and accurate knowledge.

If you are devoting your odd hours to literature, it is unnecessary to make pretensions to a knowledge of chemistry. Do not be afraid to say, "I do not know." We all expect too much learning from one another, especially elders from younger people. If John can tell his father a great deal about surveying, and Mary cannot, no matter: she can tell them both a good deal about physiology.

As far as possible, in your studying or reading, group those subjects together which belong together. If you are inclined to the physical sciences, bring into your work natural philosophy, general chemistry, general physiology, biology, geology, and mineralogy. If you desire to know more of one branch of natural science, as, for example, biology, why not group zoology, conchology, anatomy, physiology, botany, microscopy? I would always be careful not to make the group too large, though learning from one science helps in another.

This grouping system is admirable. I believe that an honest observer of the highest institutions for learning in our land, whether they were founded for the interests of young men or young women, will remark that there is too small a chance for grouping studies, and that the opportunities for choosing electives are too few. The American idea is, to get through the academy or college, and graduate with a diploma, rather than to pursue a study till such time as those who know most about that branch of learning shall deem a student ready for entrance upon higher work. I must think the German universities superior to ours in this respect. Life is short, and we can learn but little. I do not understand why it is necessary to spend several years in the preparation of certain studies for entrance to a college, when there will be no special use made of them after matriculation. I do not see how the imperative pursuit of science, for example, in school or college, is going to help the girl who is determined to devote future years to literature. Why, of course, it will not harm her; but why not be more economical of time and strength?

I can see, and know from experience, that the elective system is not wholly practical in high schools, nor for girls and boys who are not yet eighteen years old: because boys and girls need a stated amount of general knowledge, which they get in the high schools; because they are not sufficiently decided in their own minds and feelings,--not sufficiently developed, mentally, to really know what is best for them to study; and because so many boys and girls will shirk the hardest studies. I believe college presidents give these reasons sometimes in regard to their own students. But it is to me incomprehensible that men and women in college should not know what they are there for. If they are working for the name of being college graduates, it is no matter whether electives are presented to them or not. If they have not any preferences in their studies, they never will have in life. If they wish for a general broad education, which fits a student for no special position, but makes him abler to fill any place in after years, then only is a general, rather than a particular, course to be recommended. In this last case, the counsel of teachers and friends is indispensable; but, even here, choice is necessary.

But, girls, I am talking chiefly to those among you who have left the high school or academy, and have reached an age when you have ideas of your own. I shall be glad when it is possible, in the college or the home, for every girl, who wishes, to follow, special or grouped studies; and when she will no longer censure herself because, outside of elementary knowledge of it, she is not acquainted with the study her neighbor is pursuing.

In the programme of the new Bryn Mawr College, I have noted, with a feeling of satisfaction, the strong recommendations to follow grouped studies. If I understand the calendar of the University of Michigan, and the register of Cornell University, I find in these institutions a broad chance for taking electives and studies which properly belong together. These should be high commendations.

There is as much to be said on how to study as on what to study, yet I believe the question may be briefly answered. Study so that the ideas of authors may become your own, though remoulded into such forms as your own character, reason, experience and highest thoughts allow. Suppose you are studying English literature. Be watchful, first, for the writer's ideas: be sure you get *his* thoughts, not such as some one else says are his, according to some one's else interpretation; then observe the manner in which those ideas are expressed. The merits of a literary work lie quite as much in style as in the thoughts which it contains. The cause or purpose of a book, the thoughts it holds, its suggestiveness, its style, seem to me important points to bear in mind when reading or studying a work.

You may be reading George Eliot's "Romola." Be sure, when the book ends, that you see somewhat the purpose for which it was written. Be impressed with its story: follow its wonderful descriptions, its analysis of character; remark the knowledge which was brought to bear in representing that great historical character Savonarola, the Florentine republic, and the rule of the De Medicis; be moved by the pathos of the story, its dignity and beauty; but remember most, that she who begins with virtue grows, though through fiery furnaces of tribulation, into a radiant, clear, crystal womanhood.

Perhaps you are reading Dowden's "Life of Southey." Be delighted with the ease, the charm, of Dowden's style: dwell upon it. Consider his fine powers as a biographer, but be impressed with the unsurpassed diligence of Southey's life.

Are you reading Emerson's shorter essay on "Nature"? So peruse it that, when you go out among the trees and grass and flowers, you will feel the same kinship with them as did he.

History and biography, the sketch and criticism even, have been made truly charming of late years by the vividness in which actions have been depicted and characters portrayed, as well as by clearness and beauty in expression. We turn to an historical work with as much zest as to a romance, and find in it, now, that enthusiasm, that liveliness, that interest in human affairs which old historians allowed to be obscured by dates and names. If you are studying Roman history, be never so particular about when each battle was fought as about the great causes of the rise of Rome,--energy, pride, deprivation, hardihood, union of citizens, sturdiness, ferocious perseverance, courage, abstinence, valor: remark the results attained by these qualities,-- Rome, the mistress of the world, with an empire stretching to the ends of the earth. Then note the causes of her fall,--greediness, wealth, luxury, effeminacy, satiety, corrupt morals,--and bring the lesson home to your own nation, and to your own selves. Says Mr. Ruskin, "It is of little consequence how many positions of cities a woman knows, or how many dates of events, or how many names of celebrated persons--it is not the object of education to turn a woman into a dictionary. But it is deeply necessary that she should be taught to enter with her whole personality into the history she reads,--to picture the passages of it vitally in her own bright imagination; to apprehend, with her fine instincts, the pathetic circumstances and dramatic relations which the historian too often only eclipses by his reasoning, and disconnects by his arrangement. It is for her to trace the hidden equities of divine reward, and catch sight, through the darkness, of the fateful threads of woven fire that connect error with its retribution."

If you are studying the natural sciences, so follow them that you may see more clearly the rocks, the sea, the sky, the verdure of the earth, the mountains and the valleys, the rivers and the lakes,--all the creations upon the earth, as far as you have studied them,--so that a new heaven and a new earth shall be spread before you, and you shall learn to appreciate more fully the beneficence of God.

Are mathematics your choice? Then learn from them the value of stability, fixedness; the worth of accuracy in all studies and in all callings; the power of durability, especially as it refers to the durableness of right against wrong; the perfections of forms and symbols; the truths of reasoning; the necessity of discipline.

Are you translating from this or that author? Be sure that you are first accurate; then, that you have entered into the spirit of the writer and the work, that your own language is being made more copious, and fluency of speech or written discourse acquired. The discipline of translating accurately is next in value to that obtained from the study of numbers. The difficulty of turning this accurate translation into the idiom of one's own language is most stubborn.

It would be very pleasant for us to talk about the choice of books we ought to make in our reading, and I think it would be quite profitable to hunt up those authorities who have given most attention to the subject of reading. There are many such authorities.

David Pryde, in his practical papers called "The Highways of Literature," thinks the true method of dealing with books is, "(1) To read first the one or two great standard works in each department of literature; and (2) to confine, then, our reading to that department which suits the particular bent of our mind." Then he lays down these definite rules, telling us how to read: "1. Before you begin to peruse a book, know something about the author. 2. Read the preface carefully. 3. Take a comprehensive survey of the table of contents. 4. Give your whole attention to whatever you read. 5. Be sure to note the most valuable passages as you read. 6. Write out, in your own language, a summary of the facts you have noted. 7. Apply the results of your reading to your every-day duties." These rules ought, every one of them, to be emphasized in our association with books. In my own experience, I find Number 4 of great importance, as well as Numbers 5 and 7. I would add, by way of caution, that the moment you become weary from reading, or grow nervous with studying, you should stop. Studying never does harm, but nervous excitement does. When you have puzzled your brains an hour over a problem in arithmetic, the probability is that you have ceased thinking rationally, and are only plunging deeper and deeper into confusion. Nervous prostration comes from unreasonable taxation of the brain oftener than from real, systematic study.

I think you will find a little book by Charles F. Richardson very helpful in regard to your reading. It is called "The Choice of Books," and it treats of such subjects as, "What Books to Read," "How Much to Read," "What Books to Own," "The Motive of Reading," and other topics of a similar nature.

It will make an agreeable conclusion to our thoughts on what to read, and how to read, to quote the following from Richardson: "Homer, Plutarch, Herodotus, and Plato; Virgil, Livy, and Tacitus; Dante, Tasso, and Petrarch; Cervantes; Thomas a Kempis; Goethe and Schiller; Chaucer, Spenser, Shakespeare, Milton, Bacon, Sir Thomas Browne, Bunyan, Addison, Gray, Scott, and Wordsworth; Hawthorne, Emerson, Motley, Longfellow, Bryant, Lowell, Holmes, and Whittier. He who reads these, and such as these, is not in serious danger of spending his time amiss. But not even such a list as this is to be received as a necessity by every reader. One may find Cowper more profitable than Wordsworth; to another the reading of Bancroft may be more advantageous than that of Herodotus; while a third may gain more immediate and lasting good from historical novels like Eber's 'Uarda,' or Kingsley's 'Hypatia,' than from a long and patient attempt to master Grote's 'History of Greece,' or Gibbon's 'Decline and Fall of the Roman Empire.' Each individual reader must try to determine, first of all, what is best for himself. In forming his decision, let him make the utmost use of the best guides, not forgetting that the average opinion of educated men is pretty sure to be a correct opinion; but let him never put aside his own honesty and individuality. He must choose his books as he chooses his friends, because of their integrity and helpfulness, and because of the pleasure their society gives him."

VI.
ENGLISH LITERATURE AND OTHER STUDIES.

In the majority of our higher schools, and probably in the education of most persons, a deficiency in the knowledge of English is to be remarked. Now, if girls are not fond of science, nor inclined to the study of philosophy, foreign languages, music, or painting, why do they not follow certain courses in English? Why do they not study English literature, paying heed to its history, its rhetoric, but more especially to the works of its greatest authors? Literature is the most cultivating to the mind, the most necessary to a general education, and it affords the most pleasure to persons, no matter what their condition may be. Easily pursued, it requires no capital but time, and costs no more than a walk to the public library. The liberal educations which some persons have acquired from what they have read in English literature demanded only wise choice of books, time, and perseverance.

I find, on an examination of the requirements for entrance to college, that English is the least regarded. It rarely goes beyond spelling, punctuation, figures of speech, and the reading of prescribed books, few in number, and which do not require a month's study. The absurdity of demanding all the rules of Latin prosody, when the student never read a line of the "Deserted Village," and probably will not, through his college course! Says one catalogue, which represents a great institution, "A large proportion of those who seek admission to the university are found to be very deficient in their preparation in English." It is not surprising. May they be helped before they graduate from the university.

In looking over the catalogues of numerous colleges where girls are educated, I have been indeed gratified with the great advantages they present to young women. How I wish I could enjoy even a few of these privileges,--these opportunities for a higher education! Is it not much to be grateful for, that so many of you girls not only can go to college, but really do go? I am glad for you all. Smith and Wellesley, Boston University and the Annex at Cambridge, Michigan University, Cornell, Bryn Mawr, and the rest, are all magnificent attractions to the student. Yes, indeed! But how I wish that English--English literature--was more earnestly pursued in every one of them!

Within the limits of this talk, I can say but little on the study of English; so I shall confine my suggestions to a few courses of reading, which I hope may be helpful to some of you.

A knowledge of literature implies an actual acquaintance with the works of authors; and no lists of names and dates, no anecdotes, nor literary gossip, can take the place of this acquaintance: but, to make these works more useful and intelligible, we should connect history with them. How can I fully appreciate the oratory of the American Revolution, if I know nothing of the war between England and the Colonies? How can I get the real value out of "The Talisman," "Kenilworth," or "Ivanhoe," if I have no knowledge of the Crusades, of Elizabeth's reign, or of that period in English history when Richard of the Lion Heart was king? Again, how can I understand why any age in English prose or poetry was characterized by a peculiar kind of thinkers, if I do not know the history and tendency of that age? Why, in one epoch, do we have men writing on classical subjects in a way which represents form as more important than matter? and why, in another age, are writers turning from an artificial to a natural style?

Experience proves that it is profitless to study the formative periods of English literature before trying to get acquainted with it in its present condition. One should work backwards, and not forwards, in this study. The practice of beginning with Anglo-Saxon writers, and studying down to nineteenth-century authors, is to be utterly condemned. How can I hope to like or even comprehend an English version of Caedmon, or, later, Chaucer, if I cannot yet see the beauty of Whittier? The history and philosophy of English literature are indeed important, but they are entirely subordinate to the works themselves.

English literature was not hatched full-fledged; its feathers have been growing for centuries; it did not even fly high till Elizabeth's reign; and it has not been prolific till within a century or two. We want to see what the bird looks like full grown, before we can understand about the embryo in the egg.

In the first place, I should get familiar with some very concise manual, so that I might refer to it for guidance; but my most earnest work should be with certain epochs in literature, and with special representative authors, around whom I could group other dependent writers, or such as did not so nearly represent the period I was studying.

If you are studying epochwise, why not read choice selections from the prose of the nineteenth century,--some of its masterpieces? Get a general notion of the earlier parts of the century by consulting some manual on the subject, such as Spalding's "English Literature," chapters XIII., XV., and XVI. When you have ascertained that the reviews founded in the first quarter of the century contained the most valuable literature, read some of the papers in the "Edinburgh Review," the "Quarterly," and "Blackwoods." Very good collections have been made from them, especially in a series of books known as "Modern British Essayists." Read, for example, Sydney Smith's essay on "Female Education"; one of Jeffrey's criticisms on the early poets of this century; an historical or a biographical article by Alison; or one of Professor Wilson's sketches in his "Recreations of Christopher North." But be most desirous of reading that brilliant essayist, and that most impressive of contributors to the "Edinburgh Review,"-- Macaulay. I wish you would read his articles which have special reference to literature, perhaps in this order: Moore's "Life of Byron," "Mme. D'Arblay," "Goldsmith," "Samuel Johnson," "Addison," "Dryden," "Leigh Hunt," "Bunyan," "Milton," "Bacon." Of miscellaneous essays, please note "Von Ranke," "Warren Hastings," and "Frederick the Great."

After Macaulay, study Carlyle, though only in parts, reading "Heroes and Hero Worship," and "Burns." The last is especially valuable to you. Note Carlyle's sincerity, his "gospel of work," his love of Nature, his earnestness, his despair, his giant intellect. If you are interested in his peculiar merits, read the "French Revolution."

Read selections from Emerson; but always slowly, carefully, dwelling longest on this writer's more practical essays, those which inspire impulses within you to nobler living.

Realizing how great an influence Nature has exerted over the prose as well as the poetry of this century, study Emerson's two essays on "Nature"; selections from Thoreau, especially from "Excursions"; Kingsley's "Winter Garden"; passages from Ruskin, particularly those written about "The Sky," "Clouds," "Water," "Mountains," "Grass."

You will appreciate the critical spirit of this age. Though most of the authors so far mentioned were critics, as well as essayists, you will find it helpful to read from the following: De Quincey, Hazlitt, Hallam, Ruskin, Whipple. If you can read but one work from DeQuincey, take, instead of a criticism, his "Confessions of an English Opium Eater," the style of which is considered masterly. Its sentences are melodious, its English elegant and classical. From Ruskin, that writer who founded art criticism, read those delightful passages brought together in the volume called "The True and the Beautiful"; and carefully peruse the little book known as "Sesame and Lilies." Hallam I should refer to for special information in regard to European literature. Our own Whipple will aid you to a knowledge of Elizabethan learning.

Next, read the essays of Lamb, such as are included in "Elia." Love the quaint, beautiful spirit of the author; and take delight in his witticisms, his reveries, and playful fancies.

Perhaps, just here, it would be well to introduce Irving. Pay especial heed to his "Sketch-Book," "The Alhambra," and "Bracebridge Hall." In order to appreciate the position this writer holds in American literature, and the feeling with which he is regarded, both in our own country and abroad, get some knowledge of the condition of our literature before Irving placed it upon a firm basis, and learn about the grace and dignity of this man's deportment. Appreciate, too, the beauties of this author's style in writing.

Then examine the sketch as it appears in Leigh Hunt's "Wishing Cap Papers," Thackeray's "Roundabout Papers," Curtis's "Potiphar Papers." You might include under this head such rare bits of prose as you cannot conveniently classify, as, for example, Dr. Brown's "Rab and His Friends," Curtis's "Prue and I."

Now look a while at the uses of biography. I think the study of every great author's works should be either prefaced or supplemented by a good biography or correspondence. This necessary aid to literature has been amply afforded by the celebrated "English Men of Letters" series, and also by the "American Men of Letters." The influence of biographies upon your lives you will find of the highest importance. There are other lives than those of purely literary men and women which I should recommend.

You must have become aware of the great value of historical literature in this age. Note what additions it has received from the intellects of such historians as Macaulay, by his "Life of Frederick the Great" and by his "History of England"; as Motley, by his "Dutch Republic"; as Prescott, by his "Ferdinand and Isabella"; as Alison, by his "History of Europe"; as Froude, by his "Life of Caesar." One can hardly be without such valuable reference-books as Green's "History of England," Freeman's various histories, and those included in the Epoch Series. But, before reading any of these works, it would be well to read various essays on how history should be written. There is an article by Macaulay on this subject, very brilliantly written, and truthfully. There are also valuable essays on the same subject by Froude, Freeman, Carlyle, Emerson, Miss Cleveland.

You might profitably combine with this topic of history that of travels. You know works of travel form a large, and certainly a delightful, part of our reading.

You have doubtless noticed the popularity which fiction always receives. It embraces the majority of the books written in this age. Try to study, in a concise way, the development of the novel from the time of Richardson and his immediate followers, and find its most perfect expression in the works of George Eliot, Dickens, Thackeray, Hawthorne. Look a little at the history of the romance previous to this century, beginning, if you like, away back with Thomas Malory's "Morte d'Arthur." Find the best illustration of the romance in Scott. To such a writer as Scott you might add Cooper and Kingsley, though the romance is presented by the last writer in but one powerful book, "Westward, Ho!"-- at least, it seems so to me. Novelists always require a very just choice of their works. If you start with a novel of Dickens which does not lead you gradually into an appreciation of his genius, you will throw the book away in disgust. One needs to be particular about the order in which one reads Thackeray, or Scott, or Cooper, or Kingsley, even. I think the same may be said of Hawthorne.

In whatever good novel you read, be as careful to notice the artistic merits of the work, the beauties and graces of its style, as the construction of its story.

If you prefer to study the poetry of this century, you should strive first to gain a knowledge of that which was written in the last quarter of the eighteenth century. You should remark the great changes produced in the minds of writers by the French Revolution, and note the growing love for freedom of opinion and freedom in government; also the increasing love for the natural world. Then you are ready to begin with a programme like this:--

1. A General Survey of Poetry in this Century.
2. The Study of Nature and Man.
3. Wordsworth and his Poetry.
4. The Imaginative,--Coleridge's "Ancient Mariner."
5. The third Lake Poet,--Southey.
6. The History of the Ballad.
7. Campbell.
8. The Narrative,--Scott's Poems.
9. Byron's "Childe Harold."
10. The Melodies of Moore.
11. A Study of the Beautiful,--Keats and Shelley.
12. Various Secondary Poets accomplished in Verse.
13. The Song Writers.
14. The Victorian Era.
15. Tennyson.
16. Woman as Poet,--Mrs. Browning.
17. Humor in Verse,--Hood, Holmes.
18. Poetry in America,--Bryant.
19. Longfellow and Whittier.
20. Lowell and Taylor.
21. Robert Browning.

How delightful it would be to follow a programme which should include only American writers, in either prose or poetry!

Again I feel the necessity of urging you to study these authors for the thought there is in their works, and for the style in which those thoughts are expressed. Make these works text-books and pleasure-books.

If you should wish in a more general way to get acquainted with such specimens of English as combine the best style with the best matter, or with such as present either excellency in thought, or beauty in form, you might find help in the following selections. I have culled their titles, for the most part, from the catalogues of our leading schools and colleges:--

Chaucer's "Clerk's Tale;" Shakespeare's plays, particularly "Julius Caesar," "Merchant of Venice," "Macbeth," and "The Tempest;" Milton's "Paradise Lost" and "Comus;" first five cantos of Spenser's "Faery Queen;" Goldsmith's "Deserted Village" and "She Stoops to Conquer;" Scott's "Lady of the Lake" and "Marmion;" Burns's "Cotter's Saturday Night;" Coleridge's "Ancient Mariner;" Keats' "Eve of St. Agnes;" Lowell's "Vision of Sir Launfal;" Longfellow's "Courtship of Miles Standish" and "Evangeline;" Tennyson's "Princess" and "In Memoriam;" Whittier's "Snow Bound;" Sidney's "Defence of Poesie;" Bacon's Essays; Carlyle's "Burns;" Emerson's "Eloquence;" Macaulay's essay on "Milton;" Thackeray's "Henry Esmond" and "English Humorists;" Dickens's "David Copperfield" and "Tale of Two Cities;" Scott's "Kenilworth" and "The Abbot;" George Eliot's "Silas Marner" and "Romola;" Kingsley's "Westward Ho!"; Irving's "Sketch Book;" Ruskin's "Sesame and Lilies;" Addison's De Coverley papers; "Essays of Elia;" Longfellow's "Hyperion;" Whittier's essay on "The Beautiful;" Hawthorne's "Scarlet Letter" and "Twice-Told Tales;" Thoreau's "Excursions;" Leigh Hunt's "Wishing Cap Papers;" Arthur Helps's essay "On the Art of Living with Others;" Curtis's "Potiphar Papers;" Prescott's "Last of the Incas;" Motley's "Siege of Leyden." You will observe these names are given without regard to system.

Special topics may offer themselves to your mind without reference to an epoch, as the History of Fiction, the History of the Drama; or it may often be most profitable to study the literature of a certain reign or age,--as the Age of Elizabeth, the Reign of Queen Anne, the Period of the English Reformation, the Revolutionary Period. Another way of studying literature is suggested by those who, having a general knowledge of it, devote their hours of reading chiefly to one author, as, for example, Chaucer, Shakespeare, Milton. Experience proves to me that the study of a certain number of masterpieces, around which selections of less worth may be grouped, is the most thorough way to proceed.

Intimately connected with the study of literature is the science of rhetoric. By means of it we learn to appreciate good style, we are better fitted to criticise the works we read, and are certainly made better able to correct our own faults in writing. It is indispensable to the study of English literature.

As I have already stated, history and literature are closely connected, yet it is quite possible to study history so that it will have no direct bearing upon literature.

It would be an agreeable task to map out here courses in history; but the work has been so admirably done by Professor Charles K. Adams, there is really no need of any suggestions except such as are found in his "Manual of Historical Literature." In this work you will find the names and descriptions of all the books required to get a knowledge of any historical subject. The author has also given definite courses of reading on historical subjects, including in his plan all valuable works which border upon the subjects.

In history, as in literature, the most attractive and thorough way of studying is by epochs. In this connection, the little histories known as the "Epoch Series" are most valuable. The books are divided into the two general classes of ancient and modern history. Each work attempts to give a picture of an important epoch, and to faithfully discuss the period. The series pertaining to modern history includes "The Normans and the Feudal System," "The Crusades," "The Beginning of the Middle Ages," "The Early Plantagenets," "Edward the III.," "The Era of the Protestant Revolution," "The Thirty Years' War," "The Houses of Lancaster and York," "The Age of Elizabeth," "The Fall of the Stuarts," "The Puritan Revolution," "The Age of Anne," "Frederick the Great."

I should study these subjects, and group about them such works, in history, biography, fiction, or poetry, as Professor Adams suggests.

I have not selected for special remark literature, rhetoric, and history because you are girls. If this were so, I should have followed the dictates of society, and added the study of languages. Young women and young men need no particular educational differences. It has been proved that girls are as capable of excelling in any study as boys are. Let me quote to you the following:--

"A very common belief is, that women, even when studious, are rather literary than scientific. Statistics prove either that they are changing in this regard, or that the notion is erroneous. The great majority of women at the universities of Zurich and Geneva study not letters, but science and medicine. M. Ernest Legouve reported in a recent competition for fellowships in the University of France, 'The papers of the scientific candidates were greatly superior to those of letters. This result contradicts a very general opinion, which I myself have strongly supported, that scientific studies--the abstract sciences and mathematics--must hold a subordinate place in women's education, because they are incompatible with the nature of the female intellect. We have been mistaken.' In England, Miss Ormerod has distinguished herself by her observations on insect life. Very recently a paper was read before the Mathematical Society of London by Mrs. Bryant, Sc.D., on the geometrical form of perfectly regular cell structure, illustrated by models of cube and rhombic dodecahedron. In another section, Mme. Traube Mengarini studies the function of the brain in fishes; while, in our own country, Mrs. Treat and others have made valuable progress in scientific research."[5]

5 Graphic

VII.
THE COMMONPLACE.

Commonplace! Why, what is commonplace? Were it not better to call all things ordinary, or else nothing common? I suppose the pyramids are commonplace to the Egyptians, and St. Peter's to the Romans, drawing forth no words of wonder unless on special occasions; just as the stars, in their thronging pilgrimage across the sky, elicit no remarks from us, unless one falls out of the procession; and just as the dawn comes to us unfolding the new day without our ever greeting it, unless it be heralded with pomp of crimson and gold. Travel over the world, make your path a belt around the earth, visit all that is wonderful, and see all races of people,--do this without ever thinking deeply on the objects presented to sight or mind, and all things will become commonplace, unsatisfactory, dull, dronish.

Believe me, girls, there is nothing commonplace that is worth thinking about. And, pray, has God made any object which is not worth a thought?

Are you living in a city, girls, surrounded by opportunities for improving your mental faculties; blessed by association with persons of refinement; favored with that peculiar culture which only great cities can freely offer in their art-galleries, their museums, their lecture-rooms; and stimulated to do good to the poor about your streets? You are, indeed, favored: your lot is an enviable one.

Do you live out of town, and quite removed from the attractions of a metropolis? Ah! your home, then, is under clearer skies, which the city artists can only imitate; you live amidst the decorations which highest Nature imparts but to country landscapes. Without the especial occupations of city life, you escape its rush and tumult. You are being taught by slower, yet as attractive, methods, the grand lessons of life. The instruction which comes from woods and streams and hills, and the intercourse which arises among hearty country people, are more thorough and more cordial than the brick walls and hurrying crowds of a city can afford. Your chances for even aesthetic culture are not to be despised. Though you see fewer objects of art, listen to fewer men of genius, perhaps are obliged to be less among books, you learn to know the artistic works more truly, you appreciate the lecture more fully, and you remember the books you read longer.

Is your home by the ocean, on some sterile length of sand or rock, and amongst sea-faring people? Still, you are girls to be envied; for the sea has grand thoughts to tell you, and the rocks are full of meaning. The bracing air, the salt breeze, the impetuous beat of the sea, must arouse energy within you which even the heat of summer cannot wholly allay. Surely, the hospitable, the generous-hearted, people of your town must prove to you the worth of intercourse with them.

Considering, now, the position of a girl in her home, in society, in the world, I suppose we must make the confession that a large part of the discontent we have found among girls has arisen from dissatisfaction with their positions. Her resources, her industries, her pleasures, are all too narrow for her, the girl complains. Now, my dear girls, just think one moment! Isn't it rather your ignorance of your surroundings, your lack of effort to find out everything good and joyful in them, which have made you discontented? Don't you think you may be looking for something above your heads which really lies under your hands? Have you made the most of what you already possess? When one has seen England and France, then one is seized with an ardent desire to visit Germany, Italy, Russia, and Spain. When a girl has a watch, she feels a great longing for a diamond. The means of gratifying one wish are the surest passports to another wish. Oh, yes! it is well to be dissatisfied sometimes. It is never quite right to be fully contented, after a noble endeavor; but do let us stop, now and then, to see if our present condition, and what it brings to us, have not something in them as good as the future can offer.

Would it not be a good rule to make, never to get a new book till we have read the last one we bought; not to look at the second picture in the gallery till we have some idea of the first we see; not to climb Mount Washington till we have had the view from the hills in our own neighborhood?

But I suppose you think that persons, rather than objects, are commonplace,--that even some girls are so? Well, it may be you have the truth on your side; but

I should as soon think of commonplace flowers, or gems, or rainbows, as of commonplace girls. You remark, "Oh, she is very ordinary, is not at all interesting! She is neither cultured, rich, stylish, nor pretty. She is stupid!" Ah, girls, girls, do you really know what she is, or what she may become? A girl commonplace! Suppose she is not lively, is not fond of parties, does not use slang appropriately at all, is utterly ignorant of the last freak of fashion, and hardly knows whether her skirt is draped or plain; suppose she has, on the whole, a rather forlorn appearance, being pitifully unconscious of what is unbecoming in dress, or gait, or habit; suppose, in fact, she does not at once show you she has any special faculty,-- well, I have seen such a girl win a prejudiced person completely, and show that, though it cost patience to get acquainted with her, the acquaintance was worth every effort. A girl of this kind often takes us by surprise, and proves reliable in an emergency. Something remarkable is done, and we want to know who did it! We are amazed when we hear in answer the name of some quiet girl of whom we had never thought much, and we exclaim, "Why, I did not know she could do any thing! Where did she ever get the courage? I didn't know she had a speck of brains, or heart, or any kind of faculty,-- no brilliancy to her!"

Yes, girls, it must be charming to be brilliant, to be apt at repartee, to scatter bright remarks among a company as a queen scatters largess among the throngs on coronation day, to have a following in society who are like ladies in waiting. Oh, it must be delightful, for a while, to be a society heroine! You know just such a girl. She leads a dozen in her steps, and her remarks are quoted whenever the dozen are together. Ah, she is so much admired! The way in which she lets a stray look hang down over her forehead, the becoming toss of her head, the coquettish raising of her eyes, the shrug of her shoulders, the ring of her laugh,--the way she does every thing with her pretty face, her graceful form,--is so lovely! She is such a very "bright" girl too! Yes, "bright" is the word now used to distinguish one who is in appearance somewhat more than the average person.

But, girls, why not say that your friend is pretty, graceful, good-natured; that she dresses becomingly, is rather cultivated in her tastes; that she is confident of herself, and a little conceited and imperious; that she is quick, and ready with somewhat pert answers; and that she is seen at her best in society?

In spite of frowns and closed ears, girls, I am going to insist that all the attractions of a brilliant, or outwardly beautiful, girl are as nothing compared with the attractions of character which spring from many a plain, modest, quiet girl. Are you to wear your choicest attributes as you do your clothes? A sure, strong arm in danger, a gentle word in sorrow, an honest bit of counsel in doubt, courage in times of trial, hearty praise in periods of endeavor,--all qualities which have their origin in noble character,--you will come to feel are infinitely better than brilliancy. You will appreciate them in those from whom external beauty has departed, or you will recognize the loveliness of these characteristics in the ever-living beauty which the soul draws upon faces otherwise plain and homely. Cultivate that power of insight which will enable you to look beyond eyes and nose and mouth into the heart and soul of your friends: then you will see beauty indeed, then you will know how precious and how beautiful a woman's mind and a woman's character is. Then you will understand how the poet writes her song, how the artist paints her rose, how the musician meets out harmonies, how the teacher makes truth attractive. More than this--much more than this--will come from insight. When you have learned to look for inner beauty you will learn to make it your own. Behind your lovely faces and your beautiful forms there will be nourished the loftiest ideality of womanhood, which will make you not only comprehend the worth of another, but will help you to interpret all that is best and loveliest everywhere. It's very sweet to us to recall that such women as Alice and Phoebe Cary, Helen Hunt, Mrs. Browning, and Jean Ingelow were able to express in words such beautiful thoughts as could arise only from beautiful souls; but it is dearer yet to remember that women, whose numbers cannot be counted, are living those thoughts by daily acts. Learn to lift the cover from the casket of a woman's soul and you shall see jewels that never yet have been exposed to the glance of one who looks for them in sparkling eyes, in glowing cheeks, and radiant hair. If there is any thing most sweet and lovely, any thing which ought to distinguish one girl from another, it is character.

I wish, as a favor to your friend who now talks with you in print, since she cannot speak with you face to face,--I wish you would read an essay on "The Beautiful," to be found among the prose works of Whittier. There is such delicate admiration of womanliness in it; there is so much encouragement, so much love of that beauty which shows itself in character, rather than in form and presence; there is such an emphasis put to the truth that from the purity of our own minds and hearts come our knowledge of the beautiful, and our ability to find the beautiful every-where. "'Handsome is that handsome does!--hold up your heads, girls!'... Be good, be womanly, be gentle, generous in your sympathies, heedful of the well-being of all around you; and, my word for it, you will not lack kind words of admiration. ... Every mother's daughter of you *can* be beautiful. You can envelop yourselves in an atmosphere of moral and intellectual beauty, through which your otherwise plain faces will look forth like those of angels. Beautiful to Ledyard, stiffening in the cold of a northern winter, seemed the diminutive, smoke-stained women of Lapland, who wrapped him in their furs, and ministered to his necessities with kindness and gentle words of compassion. Lovely to the homesick heart of Park seemed the dark maids of Sego, as they sung their low and simple song of welcome beside his bed, and sought to comfort the white stranger who had 'no mother to bring him milk, and no wife to grind him corn.' Oh, talk as we may of beauty as a thing to be chiselled from marble, or wrought out on canvas!... what is it but an intellectual abstraction, after all? The heart feels a beauty of another kind. Looking through the outward environment, it discovers a deeper and more real loveliness."

Girls are so often afraid of the commonplace in people that they will not marry unless some one, with a true or false claim to distinction, offers himself. We have seen quite a company of girls charmed with the "de" or the "von" attached to a man's name. Every foreign capital can show its scores of American girls who have made themselves ridiculous by giving up property, home, American ideas, and American ways,--alas! by giving up much that stands for character,--for the sake of marry-ing a "pendant to a moustache," said moustache belonging to a worn-out title, and being in need of money to keep its ends waxed. Why, girls, just think! a hundred thousand dollars for the privilege of being called the wife of Monsieur le Comte de Rien, and of living, eventually, in an attic on the outskirts of Paris!

Why is it that if a young man has not certain points of distinction in the way he combs his hair, wears his collar, or affects the English gentleman, some of the girls hesitate about receiving his attentions?

If they do finally accept his kindness, they feel obliged to excuse his common-place appearance, and exclaim to their friends apologetically, "But, then, he is really good at heart, you know, and very agreeable!" Oh, pride is a valuable characteristic sometimes, but is one of the worst of evils when it tries to despise the ordinary.

Do you not think we should all be happier, girls, if we took more time to appreciate the commonplace? I have observed in the lives of great naturalists, that not only the stone which all other builders had rejected became the head of the corner in their temple of knowledge, but that the most patient observation of simplest things was the material out of which the edifice was made. Thoreau wanted to account for the fact that when a pine grove is cut down an oak forest often grows up; so he went, each year, to visit a pine lot in Concord. In his earliest observations he could see nothing except pines; but, burrowing around in the leaf-mould, he found, at last, tiny oaks an inch or two high. Year after year he visited the grove; still he could observe no special growth of the oaks. Finally the grove was cut down. Up sprang the tiny oaks, and flourished in the light and sunshine now freely admitted to them. Thick and tall, they grew into a very forest, and the pines had never a chance to rise up and crowd them out. Do you think the naturalist's search stopped then? Oh, no! He next found out how the tiny oaks came among the pines; he inquired into the habits of squirrels as planters, into the character of winds and birds as farmers and bundle-boys; and was at length able to account for the succession of our forest trees.

The commonplace will never advance to meet us; but have faith in its intrinsic merit, look for beauty, and you will find it. Could you predict that from the plants lying in the stagnant pool such a perfect flower as a lily would spring? If you were passing a low, thatched cottage made of rough stone, its only pretence being a coat of whitewash, would you guess it held a poet? And, if you were riding along in a horse-car, interested only in the foreign-looking faces and the remarkable clothes, would you be likely to know that a great philanthropist sat beside you? No, not unless you had learned to observe more wisely than most girls; and not unless you had found out the noble worth of certain ordinary men and women whose faces are not pictured in books, nor raised on medallions.

How cautious we ought to be in forming our judgments! Have you never made the mistake of replying carelessly to one whom you thought was stupid, but whom you discovered to be a person of marked ability? The older we grow, the more we are amazed at our lack of good sense in framing an opinion of those whom we meet. We are so frequently surprised at what persons do or become, we feel we can never be sure that any one is common, or of the every-day sort. We almost believe Novalis speaks the truth when he says, "We touch Heaven when we touch a human body." Let us remember then, girls, not to trust our first impressions. In forming our judgments let us be very sure our knowledge is sufficient to tell which are the sheep and which are the goats, before we begin to separate them.

Just once more let me insist on the necessity of training the observation for enjoyment of the commonplace. We call things stupid, dronish, monotonous, because our faculties are not sufficiently exercised to see any other qualities in them. Do you not suppose an artist sees more in a birch swamp than we do? Is not even he likelier to be successful in painting new wonders in the commonplace than in trying to show objects we seldom see?

Have you never noticed Albrecht Durer's drawing of Praying Hands? Look at a photograph of it, please. Is it not wonderful? We cannot describe all the feeling those hands suggest. If you had passed them on the street, you would not have noticed them, unless to remark that they were grimy, perhaps, or lean. The great German artist saw them folded in prayer, and heard all the language of a despairing soul as it came out in the expression of those hands,--wonderful hands, "instinct with spirit." Look at them again, girls.

We talked about commonplace duties when we spoke of work. Let me repeat here that life is made up of commonplace deeds. We do not have great national disturbances every day; and the surest proof that we have greater need of common events rather than startling ones, ordinary duties rather than extraordinary, is, that the moment we scorn an ordinary occurrence, or omit a daily duty, we find ourselves and every one else miserable, for a while, at least. We are stopping a part of the machinery necessary to human happiness. Let us not despise the lowliest duties. George Macdonald, the writer who has given strength to the souls of so many people, was contented to write, "If I can put one touch of a rosy sunset into the life of any man or woman, I shall feel that I have worked with God."

Do you begin to think, girls, I would have you always prosaic, plodding, self-satisfied, unambitious? Oh, no! do not understand me so. Why, I believe that even dreaming about doing, and seeing, and having things is sometimes very helpful, and not at all inconsistent with the commonplace. It is almost necessary for some people to build air-castles. They get more real pleasure in them than they would from real castles on the Rhine, the Danube, or along the rivers of sunny France. Have you never read Curtis's "Prue and I"?

Ah, how beautiful it is to be dreaming about a future, though it may never come true!--to be floating on the sunset tide of Venice; to be journeying over the passes of the Alps in summer, and always approaching Mount Blanc; to be resting by the fountain in Alhambra's Court of Lions; to be gazing at the Sistine Madonna in Dresden, or at the Ascension in the Vatican; to be dosing in an orange grove in southern California; to be awed by the deep canons of the Colorado, or to be filled with the sublimity of the Yosemite!

How glorious to be dreaming of what we will do when we are women with wills and purses all our own!--with long rows of books in our libraries, elegant pictures in our drawing-rooms, and oh! such beautiful boudoirs, all, all of our own; or, at least, a room which shall be a ***sanctum sanctorum***, where the fire on the hearth never smoulders, and where loving friends, beautiful mementos, and peaceful thoughts make us always happy. How fine to fancy longings achieved, and present desires gratified!

All dreams, yes; but they do sometimes come out better than true. The only thing wiser than dreaming is doing,--working in such a way as to bring the distant near, and getting out of the veriest commonplaces the joy we fancied lay only in the future, in other lands, or only in dreams.

Build castles and dwellings out of the commonplace, and you shall see them shine with splendor, and glow with beauties which can never be exhausted. She alone is rich who has estates in her soul.

VIII.
MOODS.

Blues, dumps, megrims, odd spells,--do they ever visit you? Drive them out of doors; chase them down the yard, over the fence, up the tree, till they go riding off on their own broomsticks, or vanish in thin air! If ever they come tapping on your window-pane again, don't open the casement; but turn your backs, stop up your ears, laugh as loud as you can, then seize the first piece of work which waits to be done. These demons are afraid of a laugh; and when they have the least suspicion that a smile wreathes the lips of a mortal, they will slink away and coil up in remote corners. They are equally alarmed by work, because it puts an armor of steel all over their opponents. This coat of mail is absolutely impenetrable, though blue imps should hurl their arrows of torture forever.

But, beware! Do not stop to think work and good cheer will put these creatures to flight. Sing your song, laugh your laugh, and make work, if none is at hand. Then only will these poor miserable prowlers shrivel up and crawl under ground.

What are gloomy moods good for? What are they not bad for? Why are we always making excuse for entertaining such company? If we are ashamed of them, let's send them packing, as we would any disreputable visitors, such as cheats, biting dogs, or poisonous insects.

How weak is our apology for enduring moods, when we blame some person, long since dead, for handing down to us an inheritance of megrims! We need not accept such a legacy, though of course we must fight very hard to resist its allurements. It may be convenient enough to censure inheritance for this or that oddity. Our grandmothers had strange moods,--spoke to people on some days and did not speak on other days,--so we have diligently doubled our bequest, and have spells odder yet,--find our friends quite delightful for a week or more, and then as distasteful for a still longer time.

The patrimony of evil can be, and will be, shamefully increased with every new generation, if good sense, sound principles, and a cheerful heart do not constantly defend the right and strive to annihilate inheritance. I am not going to discuss this matter of inheritance, girls, for there is much in it not well for us to consider at present. We are simply to remember to preserve and increase the good left us, and fight to the utmost all evil that may have come from ancestry. Every girl has peculiar forms of temptation; and what is hard for one to resist is easy for another to repel, because to the latter it is no temptation. If moods, grim moods, are worth any thing to us, they are simply worth conquering,--merely valuable for the strength we get from their defeat.

Plainly, it is our selfishness, our indulgence, our idleness, our vanity, which make us allow such wretched company within our walls.

See what wily creatures the *blues* are!--full of conceit! They grow powerful while looking at us. They are like those little wood creatures which can take the hue of the tree on which they rest, so that for a long time we do not perceive them. They sit beside us by hundreds when we fancy we are alone; and change their colors and their wheedling tones to suit our inclinations, while they pour into our ears deceitful whisperings that the world is all wrong, and we are all right,--the vile flatterers! They paint all our surroundings with dark colors, make all our pictures Mater Dolorosas or St. Sebastians, turn all our music into requiems, and all our books into Stygian epics.

I cannot think there is any thing much more destructive to human happiness than the *blues*. I wonder how they ever came by their name? It must have arisen from the weirdness of the tempest, from the changing hues of the snake's skin and the lizard's back, from the blue of sharp steel, from lighted brimstone, and from driving sleet.

Now, girls, why do you, of all people in the world, allow yourselves to be mastered by freaks? Do you not have troubles? Of course you do,--real troubles, which are full of pain and discouragement. Your feelings are so acute, you are so susceptible, I do not see why a sorrow should not be deep with you. But with your vigor, your pure affection, your generous impulses, with all the future before you in which to keep on trying, I cannot understand why you should hug such a phantom as a mood. Just think again how dangerous gloomy moods are,--how bold! Why, with the least hint at an invitation, they will come in, not for a call, nor for one meal, but to stay and stay,--the impudent creatures! And such despoilers as they are while they remain! They eat you out of house and home, they even take away your own appetite,--the harpies! They make you cross,--yes, ugly. They bring frowns, tears, and age into your faces, and they banish all loveliness to the ends of the earth. Oh, do *not* let them in!

When you come home tired out, your energy all gone, your patience exhausted, why,--rest. Do not think you are desolate, that everybody has deserted you, and that fate, destiny, grim despair, are all after you. You are tired and need to go to bed, or to engage in some light talk which will rest you but at the same time occupy you. Read the newspaper, build aircastles, hope with all the combined powers of your fancy. If the clouds of misfortune pile up, and it pours bad luck,--mother scolds because you did not sweep your room carefully; father threatens because of an approach to familiarity with the new young man over the way; brother frets because his stockings are not well darned; lessons all went wrong in the morning; your best friend said a careless word to you; you have broken the main-spring of your watch, and spilt coffee on your new dress,--why, these are all trifles! I know a good many bad trifles coming together are worse than a misfortune; but the best way to prevent them from bringing on dejection is to let in such a flood of light and determined cheerfulness as to drown out despair.

Mr. Emerson, in an essay on "Behavior," tells a capital story about a man who was so bent on being cheerful he put to shame the torments of hell itself. "It is related of the monk Basle, that, being excommunicated by the Pope, he was, at his death, sent in charge of an angel to find a fit place of suffering in hell; but, such was the eloquence and good humor of the monk, that wherever he went he was received gladly, and civilly treated, even by the most uncivil angels; and, when he came to discourse with them, instead of contradicting or forcing him, they took his part, and adopted his manners, and even good angels came from far to see him, and take up their abode with him. The angel that was sent to find a place of torment for him attempted to remove him to a worse pit, but with no better success; for such was the contented spirit of the monk, that he found something to praise in every place and company, though in hell, and made a kind of heaven of it. At last the escorting angel returned with his prisoner to them that sent him, saying that no phlegethon could be found that would burn him; for that, in whatever condition, Basle remained incorrigibly Basle. The legend says his sentence was remitted, and he was allowed to go into heaven, and was canonized as a saint."

Do not give away one day to despair: better lose it in idleness. When friends seem careless of you, when poverty encroaches, when suffering ensues from wrongs others have done, when sickness or any kind of calamity besets you, and when you are hunted to the verge of gloom, cling to the ropes which hope suspends about you, and they will surely pull you back from the abyss. These trials all have their uses.

And, pray, be mindful of the way you look at things. Do not try to see evil: have on your kind eyes, magnify every dot of goodness. "In all things throughout the world, the men who, look for the crooked will see the crooked, and the men who look for the straight will see the straight."[6] Try especially to see what is good in your own lot. If you have not fine carpets, luxurious chairs, fresh bouquets every morning, remember you can better appreciate a cane- seated rocker when you are tired, a well-swept floor which has a rug or two, and a single flower purchased with well-earned money.

As I suggested in the beginning, work is as sure a cure for dejection as cheerfulness is. Why, I have seen one hour's solid labor eat up all the blue tribe which had been hatching and hatching by millions. Sometime will you read from Carlyle's "Past and Present" his chapters on work, particularly that on "Labor and Reward"? Mr. Carlyle has written much that is unintelligible to most readers. He has a very grotesque, volcanic style not good to imitate. He is often sad and hopeless about the human race, but he knew from hard experience what work could do against despair. So, in spite of his ravings, notwithstanding his eruptive style, and his sorrow for what is, he has given us, in a masterly piece of prose, this noble "Gospel of Work."

His sentences, alive with enthusiasm, and terrible in their seriousness, contain great reaches of thought, poetry, prophecy, like that of the ancients; and all are full of the praises and rewards of labor. "Consider how, even in the meanest sorts of labor, the whole soul of a man is composed into a kind of real harmony the instant he sets himself to work! Doubt, Desire, Sorrow, Remorse, Indignation, Despair itself, all these like hell-dogs lie beleaguering the soul of the poor day-worker, as of every man; but he bends himself with free valor against his task, and all these are stilled, all these shrink murmuring far off into their caves. The man is now a man. The blessed glow of labor in him, is it not as purifying fire, wherein all poison is burnt up, and of sour smoke itself there is made bright, blessed flame!" "Doubt of any kind can be ended by action alone."

What makes us blame the weather so much for our moods, girls? The day is gray everywhere,--in the skies, on the trees, in the air, on the ground,--and gray in us therefore. Ah! but these gray colors are beautiful, even in November and December. In their variety they are soft and shimmering on the tree branches, a slightly ruddy gray on the branchlets, and a serener gray on the tree trunks. Overhead, even when a storm is gathering in the sky, there are the colors of the moonstone tinting into silver, and shading into pearl and blue. On the ground are delicate wood-colors,--umbers, siennas, greens toned down to gray. The atmosphere, from its lack of sunlight, only sets off the more visibly beautiful forms of trees and branches.

No, the day is not moody: we are. We are not in harmony with her, but have arrayed our-selves against her. "When we are at one with Nature we have great peace; when fretted and unmindful of her presence, we are irritated, and out of our true element." In our megrims we have found something whose defenceless condition we think ought to bear the burden of our misery.

Well for you the weather affords a chance for an excuse; for a moody girl on a bright June morning, when all Nature is radiant with beauty, is the veriest parody on life,--worse than that, a sad mockery.

If you are very sensitive, do not censure yourselves too severely, nor foster distrust; for the latter is worse for you than self-conceit.

Be sure to make the *blues* as dangerous as possible; be always mindful of their direful attacks.

Some one asks me, just here, if she is never to feel serious? Of course she is to have very thoughtful hours! The merely gay, happy-go-lucky kind of a girl is not the most helpful, nor the most valuable. There is very deep happiness sometimes in thoughtfulness,--do you not know it? What makes you quiet when you row in and out of the shadow-filled coves along the river-border, or when you drift among the islands purple with sunset light? What makes you want to shut your eyes, and to throw away the mask of seeming, when some one sings the song you love? and what makes you feel a kind of dead, low, dreadful pause, when the reader's voice ceases, and the story conies to an end? Are you moody? No; only resting. Your being is suspended in thought,--thought so serious yet so delicate, so subtle, you cannot weave it into words. Sometimes, to be sure, a girl who is determined to be morbid will distort such serene feelings into moodiness; but, then, these sudden spells of dejection are only distantly related to the real blue urchins.

Perhaps, girls, it will be better for you if you make up your minds early in life that your lot will probably be about like that of the average girl,--that trouble must come, and even a skeleton must hang and gibber behind your door; but that, be the skeleton what it may, you will nail the door back on the unsightly thing, clothe it in some decent garments, and make it as respectable as possible in its niche, since it must stay with you. Events, decrees, circumstances, will not change for just you and me; but we can change ourselves, and so defeat them. Do not mind untoward circumstances. "Seize hold of God's hand, and look full in the face of His creation, and there is nothing He will not enable you to achieve." A crust with contentment is better than a pudding with the bitter sauce of discontent.

Oh, I know, girls, it sounds very much like dull preaching. But, really, do we enjoy moods? Do we have any respect for ourselves while in them? Aren't we always trying to blame some one else? Shocking business, hunting up scape-goats!

Just see how you look when you have given place to these evils. You respect beauty: you would resent any criticism on your personal appearance at a party; but if one should truly describe how careless, how unmindful of beauty in looks or beauty in disposition, how ugly you are, when in this deplorably moody state, you would shun your very self, and want to get out of your body somehow. You watch a girl who has an attack of the megrims. She seems to hang from her shoulders, or thereabouts; her nimbleness is gone; her muscles seem flabby; she reels more than she walks; she picks up a book to let it fall down; she will not look her neighbor in the face; the meaning has all gone out of her eyes; her mouth is the only expressive feature; her lips are either tightly pressed or curled in scorn; there is a don't-care look all over her, and it lurks in the folds of her dress, in her slouching hat, her unbuttoned coat, and in her shambling gait.

Sometimes the picture is quite the reverse. The muscles seem tense and powerful. The eye is set and firm, ferocious in fullness. The step is quick and heavy. The strength is doubled, and every object has to yield to the ugliness which attacks it. The form appears to gather passion more and more with each hour, till, at last, full of violence, the human frame sways, heaves, and the girl breaks her mood into a flood of scalding tears. The contest is fierce while it lasts. It is dreadful to see beauty put on such deformity, but let us be thankful it is soon over. If the lightning does not strike anywhere, perhaps all will be clearer after the storm.

These violent squalls are not to be compared with those periods of long, low mutterings, nor with those seasons of painful silence, hours of uncertainty, which at times cloud so many girls. Why, the moods of some persons are like yellow days, dark days, and judgment days. A girl shuts herself up for an afternoon, for a day, for two days A stone sepulchre is all about her, and she only reaches out of it when she wants bread and water. She, herself, does not seem to be in her body: she is a ghost. When we pass by her tomb-like body, perhaps a head will nod to us, or lips will mutter monosyllables. If our dress touches her garments we feel like begging pardon, A kind of horror and at the same time a sort of pity invade us, yet we are paralyzed and cannot help her. I hardly think the word is employed by lexicographers with this meaning, and I apologize for using the expression; but this kind of an odd spell is what I call *smudging*.

It seems so strange that a girl can use her will so powerfully about controlling others, and yet remain herself the dupe of an unkind mood. To be sure, there are causes for ill-humor arising nearly every day,-- ill-health, poverty, sorrow, cares that haunt and harrow, unaccomplished desires, ungratified longings; but the indulgence of dejection, the lack of resistance to a mood, only increase hardship. How is the doctor to help your body, if you do not help your spirits? How are your surroundings to be improved, if you do not go to work? How are you to get work, if you do not seek it, and try with all your might to find it? How is trouble to be lessened or endured, if from it we do not reach to higher, nobler living? The way out of trouble is not through despair. Hope unlocks the temple doors, Despair rusts the keys. Each must know her own anxieties best; but the trials of all, we shall sometime see, are but bitter on the outside, sweet and nourishing within. Believe in the *sometime*.

IX.
WOMANLINESS.

There is something in woman fascinating to woman herself, and something in a girl irresistibly attractive to a girl herself. Mere words being unsufficient to express the emotion caused by this charm, a girl makes use of a large force of ejaculations, utters her indescribable "Oh's!" and "Ah's!" in every variety of crescendo and diminuendo, and emphasizes her pitch with gestures that point her meaning, till not the slightest doubt exists that she has been impressed by something wonderful. She does not know, indeed, just what it is that makes Sallie Henderson so delightful; but "Oh, she is per-fect-ly lovely!--too sweet for any thing!" Now I think the quality which so attracts is womanliness, the most desirable of all the gifts a girl is permitted to cultivate. All the littlenesses in the social customs of girls; all their raw, untrained, ungenerous acts, their indulgences, their prejudices, are the weak and despised signs of unwomanliness.

Womanliness is not primness, let me be understood. The straight, smooth hair, the folded hands, the demure face and exact deportment from ten years of age to eighty, do not always indicate womanliness; nor does the attempt to turn young girls into elderly women produce it. So many patchwork quilts, so many hand-stitched shirt-bosoms, so many worsted stockings, made before a girl is fourteen, are so many quilts, bosoms, and stockings more than she will make when she is forty. Hours for sewing, for helping in the home, for studying, are necessary to even children, because industry, patience, application, and system must be encouraged in earliest years; but the hours girls spend in the house doing things neatly and in order, as their grandmothers did before them, ought to be balanced by hearty exercise in the fresh air, by seasons of mirth, and by freedom from restraint. The out-of-door exercise, the gayety, the deliverance from tasks, are quite as necessary for older girls as for younger ones.

There is a value to be placed on the very trappings of girlhood which do not in the least interfere with womanliness. At sixteen or eighteen, perhaps at twenty, a girl can toss a jaunty little felt hat upon her head, pin it in a twinkling above her wayward hair, tie on a bit of blue or red somewhere about her blouse, tuck in her handkerchief in a pardonable way, brush her short walking-skirt into becoming folds, tie up her tennis shoes, and there she is in five minutes, prettier, fresher, more becomingly dressed than all the older women of the household, who have been standing before the mirror trying this effect and that for the last hour. Ask a girl how she does it, how she manages to make her hat bend down and up, and in and out, in all kinds of alluring ways, and she does not know,--it belongs to girls to do such things. Of course it does! Whatever they do must be bewilderingly charming sometimes, because they are girls. You know, when we buy choice roses from the gardener, we are always particular to select those just approaching blossom. A delicacy, and yet a richness of color and fragrance are upon them; a brightness and yet a tenderness in tone,--the bloom is there more soft and beautiful than in the fully opened rose. That bloom and color, that tenderness and dreamy softness, that richness and freshness, are yours, dear girls.

Yes, indeed! there is something charming in a girl simply because she is a girl. It is in the ring of her laugh, in her irony, in her frankness or her coyness, in the way she does the commonest things,-- puts on her scarf, or catches hold of your arm,--things that only too soon disappear in conventionalities, ceremonies, and proprieties. But there is no need of this change as concerns much that is now called only girlish. The womanly element is the main quality to be nourished into greater perfection, but only the weakness of girlishness is to be excluded from character. Girls are to grow wiser, and to avoid what must bring harm, but still to keep the attractive freshness of maidenhood. Some of the most delightful women we meet are those who can be girls with girls, and women with women. The young do not lose their respect for them because they appreciate them, nor do elders lessen their regard for these women because they have kept the loveliness of girlhood.

Girls, I am not trying to defend you: your girlhood needs no such effort; but I do want to make you all feel that the very sweetness of your natures, the loveliness of your lives and conduct, your attractive grace, which ought to strengthen with years and become something more than beautiful,--become divine,--is womanliness.

God did not make all the girls beautiful, strong, or intellectual; but He did make them all capable of becoming womanly. You may well doubt this ability the next time you see an intelligent and pretty girl avoid the glance of a former friend who is now miserable and weak; and you may question its very existence in the wretched and outcast one. Ah! but who can judge, or even know, the inner life of one's past acquaintances? It is not for you, nor for me, to slight, to scorn, to condemn the fallen. Of this we are sure,--that no beauty, no intelligence, can compare with womanliness; and that no girl, weak and wicked as she may be, is utterly lost to a return to womanliness. May I here appeal to you, dear girls, to hasten this return? May I urge you not to slight even the sinful? As you are girls with most precious endowments, remember to encourage the growth of these gifts in other girls. Then will womanhood seem even more blessed than now,-- when girls defend it and purify it. A girl may have all the privileges that a boy has; a woman, all the rights that a man now has in excess,--pray, do not let us stand in the way of such favors!--but the fact remains that "woman is not undeveloped man, but diverse"; and the one thing she owes to the world, to herself, to her Maker, is a reverence for her own sex. Girls, I repeat, you cannot sufficiently realize your obligations to your own kind. Because you are girls and not boys, women and not men, oh, try to be loyal to girls and women! Pay homage to womanhood; adorn it, place sacrifices upon its altars, rejoice in unceasing service to it, exalt it by every worthy endeavor!

This reverence for woman is the first and truest step towards womanliness. When this has not been taken, and a girl is therefore unkind to her social inferiors out of fear of what rumor will say,--"the fume of little hearts,"--I blush for an indecent girlhood, and I grieve for an unpromising, unchristian womanhood. We know that encouragement, not intimacy, the gentle rebuke of a bow or a greeting, are more helpful to arouse the sparks of womanliness than the cold stare or averted head. Next to the respect of woman for woman, comes the regard of woman for man,--a deference (when physical, mental, or spiritual strength in man demand) that is due from her who, constituted differently, has greater power to pay respect and gratitude, to honor and love. Gentlemanly boys and men have a right to expect you to be refined, courteous, agreeable towards them in all the ways of ladyhood,-

-not that they are your superiors, but your helpers: made after a different pattern, but still your sincere friends.

The womanly in girls implies the lady, no doubt, more than the manly in man indicates the gentleman. We ought always to find in girls that gentleness and delicacy of manner, that minute attention to the comforts of others, that visible respect towards others, so agreeable and so refining in all circles. Marguerite de Valois wrote, "Gentleness, cheerfulness, and urbanity are the Three Graces of manners." I believe they bear a close relation to ladylike deportment.

All can acquire these habits of politeness and attention to others, though they come not with ease to those of us whom unfavorable surroundings continually influence. A woman in an almshouse, a girl serving a ship's crew, can be a lady and not cost her masters more, though her efforts cost her much.

But, valuing all that constitutes a lady, believing that these gentle graces are necessary to every girl, I believe the ladylike is but a part of true womanliness,-- that infinitely precious, indescribable something in woman that makes her royal by birth, queen of herself, and fit to occupy the throne that is placed beside the king's throne,-- not higher, not lower, but beside it; not his, but like his; her own, from which, with equal though with differing eye, she looks in blessing on the world.

Oh, how, girls, shall we get this womanliness into our characters, or, rather, how shall we make it shine out of them? If we stop to think once in a while what it is, if we remember that it is unassuming as it is beautiful, and only waits for our acquaintance, we shall the sooner embrace it. And then, if we are reminded that it does not despise common things, lowly homes, simple pleasures, any more than it does benevolent acts, patient lives, and ordinary toils, we shall oftener be found cherishing it. Let us remember that womanliness is in our elders,--women like Susan Winstanley, of whom "Elia" tells in "Modern Gallantry." You know she was cold toward her lover, and when asked why, she replied she was perfectly willing to receive his compliments and devotion, as was her right; but that, just before he came to pay his regards, she had overheard him roughly rating a young woman who had not been quite prompt with his cravats, and she thought what a simple change of place might have caused, and said, "I was determined not to accept any fine speeches to the compromise of that sex the belonging to which was, after all, my strongest claim and title to them."

Let us remember that womanliness is in all the motherliness we see in our mothers; that it is in all the sacrifices and noble deeds of silent women, as well as in those of celebrated women, like Elizabeth Fry or Mrs. Browning; that it is in the acts of all those who make the ordinary home "like the shadow of a rock in a weary land," and a "light as of a Pharos in the stormy sea." If we are impressed with the remembrance that womanliness is in such and such characters, we shall try harder to imitate them; we shall be more thankful we are women, and more grateful that it belongs to us especially to impart what man lacks, and what he must depend on us to supply.

Here, again, I want to emphasize the fact that womanliness does not require a girl to abandon merriment, vigorous exercise of the body, or brain, or heart, freedom in sports, and "a jolly good time." But let us have every thing in its place. Kid-gloved hands in a huckleberry pasture, or on a row-boat, would be as unbecoming to a girl, you will agree, as a soiled collar in the school-room, or a dusty jacket in church. We do not object to boys sitting astride a fence: it is rather manly than otherwise, if they do not concoct a plan to tear their clothes; but it does seem a bit out of the womanly way for a girl. To be sure, there is not much difference between climbing fences and many of the gymnastic performances for girls; but time and place must be regarded. I should not frown if I heard a girl whistling, under two conditions,--she must be a good whistler, and confine her musical exercise to the woods. I think it is fine to see a girl go over a fence without sticking between the bars, and it really is too bad to have to be pulled through by an "I told you so!" It is fine to see a girl play ball or tennis; to see her row or ride, or climb a tree when there is need. But all this climbing, and striding, and shouting, womanly enough at times, become most unwomanly under certain circumstances, especially in the home.

Such indications go far to pronounce us loose in manner, immodest in deportment, coarse and vulgar, where we are not understood. No girl can afford to wilfully bring upon herself the criticism of bad manners. She can afford to do right when she feels the world is wrong; but she is accountable for her example, and the influence she exerts upon those not as strong as she is. Beyond this lies the fact that womanliness is opposed to mannishness, and that unwomanliness grows faster than its virtuous opposite. "Ill weeds grow apace," says a German proverb. One plantain in a garden will eat out not only the flowers in the plats, but the very grass in the borders. Any thing that takes away from modesty, refinement, gentleness, takes away from womanliness. Says Beaconsfield, "The girl of the period,--she sets up to be natural, and is only rude; mistakes insolence for innocence; says every thing that comes first to her lips, and thinks she is gay when she is only giddy."

I sometimes think, girls, it is the motherliness in some of you that often makes you womanly; not altogether the quality that makes little folks hug their dolls,--not altogether that,--though, in their gentle cares, their tender caresses and assumed anxieties, they are little women in themselves; but I mean, too, the motherliness that makes girls careful of others. It is an all-sheltering fondness; it is a delicate superintendence over the comforts of another; it is a brooding thought about the nestlings of one's heart, hearth, or associations; it is a cultivated instinct that smooths out difficulties, and steps right along beside purity and loveliness.

This characteristic of womanliness is not that weak, unsubstantial quality which we sometimes associate with effeminacy.

I would not imply that womanliness does not exist in those women whom superior talents have raised above the average man. A great lecturer, after holding her audience long by her eloquent appeals for reforms, stepped down into the crowd slowly departing, and earnestly inquired after this sick friend, that poor one, and the prosperity of another. The marvel of her womanliness was even more striking than the power of her oratory.

As I said at first, girls, girlishness, while inferior to womanliness, is no hindrance to it. It is most proper for girls to discuss tucks and ruffles, gloves and boots, bangs and twists. They think about these things properly enough, too, or they would not make such good use of them. They are in no danger of becoming less worthy women, provided they do not exclude thoughts on higher things. But girlishness, construed to mean just a love of dress and finery, does not make womanliness. If it did, every well-clothed girl on the street would be virtuous. I confess, however, that it would require a good deal of persuasion to make me believe that untidy skirts, buttons clinging by a thread, or utter inattention to style, to neatness and wholeness, were traits in a womanly woman.

We are told that true manliness and true womanliness are one and the same. At some points, these qualities meet and mingle. In the strongest parts of character, men and women are the same. In trying moments, in hours of great interest, in times of rare experience, men and women do the same work in the same way, and then the high quality which ennobles their characters is human kindness. It is well that great artists have painted the face of Christ so that it is as womanly as it is manly. It is a beautiful way some persons have of thinking of God as father and mother too.

But with all these resemblances of manliness to womanliness, there is a difference which all may recognize if they will. Allow a boy to stretch out his legs, climb spouts, jump gutters,--he is still perfectly manly; but a girl cannot do these things in a community without censure, unless necessity requires. I know that the custom which demands different decorum for a girl is arbitrary, and not of divine origin. To go unveiled is not allowed in some countries. But conformity is surely enjoined upon us; and that, so far as it is reasonably observed, is a really womanly trait. I cannot help thinking that girls are made of finer material than boys, but of stuff that will wear just as well as the stockier goods in boys. Inasmuch as a girl has more confided to her keeping than a boy has, she ought to be so much the more watchful. A girl ought to guard purity, modesty, patience, hope, trust, because she has had these things given her in large measure.

What can there be more beautiful than womanliness! The next time you see the Sistine Madonna, look behind all the mother in the lovely face for the woman in it. Then see if you do not remark the same in Raphael's St. Cecilia, and in the Venus de Milo, Wherever masters have succeeded in painting the Virgin, notice, aside from the holy look,--if any thing can be aside from that,--the womanly look. What is it which makes us love some women's faces the moment we see them? Sometimes it is because the loveliness of their character beautifies most ordinary features. Sometimes it is because we expect them to do some very womanly deed,--to heal us of diseases, to right wrongs, to defend causes, to uplift the fallen. Girls are not all weak and uncertain, because they are girls. No; they are strong and brave, and reliable in danger. The boiler of a steam-yacht exploded; several girls were on board; the crew were busy saving themselves; the girls, with an electric shock of mother-care, jumped to save one another. They neither fainted nor screamed, with one exception, which was a somewhat feeble serving-girl, who was stoutly shaken and told to faint if she dared.

Perhaps you think that refinement and good education produce greater womanliness than ignorance and low surroundings. So they do; but the worst of circumstances, as we have already shown, cannot crush it. There is much to be feared from over-refinement, or, rather, superficial cultivation, which breeds selfishness, vitiates strength, encourages false pride, enervates the whole life of a girl. Look at the girl half clad, sleeping in the lazy sun that falls across her narrow doorway, droning out life; now and then, in an hour of wakefulness, muttering some coarse word. And then regard the over-cultured, the wrongly-bred girl; the peevish, dictatorial, selfish, haughty miss of a certain other door-way,--a parlor-way. The womanliness in both would not amount to so much as is in one bright gleam from the eye of an Evangeline.

We cannot tell so much what womanliness *is* in girls as what it ***does***. It lies mostly in the little acts they perform,--those things which are so often done that we neglect to speak of their worth, and yet should feel most sad without them. The humblest deeds, the oft-repeated ones, form the beauty of characters and faces. They put beautiful lights into girls' eyes, softness into their cheeks, and winsomeness into the whole face. Then, too, deference to the feelings and notions of others has much to do with the sweetness of womanhood. It cannot be wrong to read a letter on the street, to shout to one's friend on the opposite side of the way, to whistle to a horse-car driver; but, so long as these offend preconceived notions of good manners, deference to the opinions of others should forbid such habits.

Now let us see, just once more, what we mean by a womanly girl. Exact attention to points of etiquette, gracefulness, accomplishments, proper subservience to the will of others, do not of themselves make womanliness; many more than these characteristics, and greater, are needful. First of all, a girl must feel she is a woman, with a heart to cultivate in its affections, restrain in its desires, curb in its selfishness; with a mind to enrich by such means as shall promote its best peculiarities, and supply its needs; with a soul to enlarge into more generous impulses, and into the performance of more worthy deeds. Such a girl looks practically, but at the same time cheerfully, on life. She is willing to make the best and most of her lot, and, though out of patience with it sometimes, is not always battling against circumstances.

Discontent, to be sure, is as unmanly as it is unwomanly; but I fear it is an ill more widely spread among girls than among boys. It is an evil seed, and brings forth nothing but choking weeds and noxious plants. No position, nothing that a girl can do, harms her, provided she be womanly; therefore, choice of position cannot help, unless she is sure she has power to do better in another place. Some servants are more womanly than the women who employ them. We are all servants to one another: each holds the mastery. Surely we must be novices before we can be superiors. In one sense, servitude is an ornament; for politeness is but a visible sign, of glad service. Surely, politeness is a real property of womanliness.

A truly womanly girl is genuine in what she says and does. Avoiding the bombast, the occasional coarseness of rougher natures, the self- esteem, and the dictatorial manner, she yet says no, when she means no. If that causes hurt, she is not slow to express her sympathy and show her sorrow. She does not do things for effect, nor to arouse unjust indignation.

If we were to study the points of character that have made women celebrated, we should find them within the power of any earnest girl to obtain through great strength of womanhood. I mean those women who have been the bravest, truest, tenderest, most loved by the world. Philippa pleading with bended knee before Edward III. to spare the lives of the men of Calais, Catherine urging her suit before Henry VIII., Madame de Stael supplicating Bonaparte for her father's liberty, Marie Antoinette ascending the steps of the scaffold, are but few of the women of history who furnish us examples of highest womanhood. Literature supplies as great illustrations: Antigone going to bury her brother's ashes in spite of the king's threat to take her life; Zenobia in chains in the midst of a great Roman triumph,--a woman still, with firm though downcast eyes; Rebecca, in "Ivanhoe," standing on the tower ready to give the fatal spring the moment Bois Guilbert should approach with dishonorable purpose,--all furnish vivid pictures of what strength of womanliness can accomplish. Simple traits caused their noblest actions,--love, sympathy, tenderness, purity, bravery, resolution, endurance; but these qualities, grown almost to their utmost, make these women dear to us. It was not intellect, it was not pride, it was not position; but it was the womanhood perfected in them that enabled them to do their work, and enables us to love and follow them.

We are under the strongest obligations, girls, to our sex, ourselves, and the world.

X.
GIRLS AND THEIR FRIENDS.

My dear girls, do not fancy that I am going to preach on friendship: so wide a theme is beyond the scope of these little talks with you. I simply wish to express a few old-fashioned opinions about girls and their friends.

Though now and then I may seem to be talking about that which is less than friendship, or that which means more, please understand I fully recognize the fact that, though acquaintance, friendship, love, often merge into one another by advancing steps of familiarity, they are really three distinct qualities.--One's acquaintances are many, one's friends comparatively few, one's lovers fewer yet,--or they ought to be. Do you know, girls, you do suggest the most delightful subjects for a talk! There is no such thing as resisting your attractive traits! But I am going to say a few very plain things about what may not be charming in you.

Girls feel very quickly. They are not in the least slow to comprehend with the heart; in fact, it often seems as though that organ were constructed with as much delicacy as is the Aeolian harp, which quivers and utters sounds when the air just stirs about it. The most of you are very emotional; and that quality of emotion, when it is pure, is your blessing, and a part of the womanhood in you: it is the necessary expression of your soul. I know the word emotional has not a pleasant sound, and, in common use, implies lack of reason and want of control; but it is a good word, and what it truly means is good. Feeling, or the product of feeling, which is emotion, does for us what reason cannot do,--it frequently causes faith where reason would destroy it. Do not boast you are not emotional, and have no care nor sympathy for fine sentiment; for this boasting is not laudable in a woman. The girl who reasons more than she feels will make a calm philosopher, but a very poor friend.

Though we are not to speak so much about God's highest gift to us,-- the power of loving,--I would like to show you just what feeling is capable of doing. You know most girls have an affection for somebody or something, and if that love is not bestowed on a friend, it will be on a cause, an ambition, an absorbing desire. Hypatia, Joan of Arc, Charlotte Corday, Florence Nightingale, Harriet Hosmer, Rosa Bonheur, Mrs. Siddons, represent as much love for the causes they lived or live for as did Vittoria Colonna for her husband, Hester and Vanessa for Swift, Heloise for Abelard, Marguerite for Faust, Ophelia for Hamlet, Desdemona for Othello, or Juliet for Romeo. These last, I repeat, were bound in the cause of love not less than the former; and they all owed their endeavors--their success, if they gained it--to the feelings and emotions of their natures.

But the trouble is, girls, you do lack judgment in the management of your feelings. It has been suggested by an able philosopher that persons differ from one another principally in the amount of judgment they possess. Really, you do not always bestow your friendship worthily, but too often let your emotions master instead of guide you; then your eyes become blind to every thing that is best for yourselves and your friends: you get selfish, passionate, and demoralized.

Hold the reins of feeling in obedience to what is good and right, no matter what the suffering is which follows. Do you remember how Irma loved the king in that grand struggle for character which Auerbach paints "On the Heights," where the full, rich nature of Irma, so capable of loving, so prone to err, yearns for the fulfilment of her longing, yet will not yield an inch of conscience when once she knows it is wrong for her to love? You know she dies struggling, but it is on the heights, where, Goethe tells us, "lies repose." There are many and many women martyrs who go to their graves unknown, suffering no pangs of the Inquisition, the gallows, or the guillotine, but tortured by unrequited affections,--by a love which it was not possible to gratify without a loss of principle or a sacrifice of conscience. Is it not better to break one's heart than to break one's soul?

My dear girls,--I would not say it were I not obliged to do so,--you seem the least conscientious in making friends, rarely thinking how grave and yet how sweet a joy a friendship is. In the first place, you seize upon a friendship as though it were something to be worn already made, like a new bonnet which pleases you. No matter what the girl is, she suits your present whims; so your swear an eternal friendship with her, when you do not begin to realize that real friendship depends upon time and growth,--that it consists largely in a mutual finding out of two persons.

Then, again, you frequently choose friends for some material advantage to yourselves. Do you think you ought to do that? You see something in a girl which you believe will promote your interests: perhaps she is in society a good deal; maybe she is very bright and sharp at repartee; possibly she is stylish, and absorbed in dress; perhaps her father has money, or she has an eligible brother,--at any rate, she can advance your purposes in one way or another, so you presume to make her your friend. Now you know you ought to value friendship for just its sake alone. If you are to make a friend, do so because you cannot honestly help it, and no strong reason exists why you should help it.

Naturally, like chooses like: some point of beauty, some mark of excellence, some trait of character, will draw us to another, because these things exist in ourselves, though undeveloped, or because we wish them to so exist; so friendship will spring up and flourish till it ripens into love. This is the best and most loyal way of making friends; and, if this be called choice, indulge in it, though not from any material profit you are to get, but simply because you are fond of one who is worthy of the best you can give her.

Then you will see that, if a girl and her traits were lovable when she and you were school-mates, they deserve to be loved still: then a year after graduation you will know the girl when you meet her on the street, and recognize her as you did in school. Girls and boys do not change so completely after leaving school. Eleanor, though in plain clothes washing up the kitchen-floor, is Eleanor still; and Frank, though only patching fences, is still Frank. Changes in circumstances and in ourselves sometimes prevent the keeping of a friend, and we no longer find friendship in the places where we used to seek for it; but inconstancy in ourselves is a greater enemy to the holding of a friendship than any external circumstance.

One great reason why certain girls of good parts remain in the same position in which their ancestors had lived--struggling with poverty, with bad tempers, with an indifferent lot, and wrestling with a savage discontent--is because they are not encouraged to any thing better when they get out of school. The free institutions of learning in the United States begin a noble work of co-education and co-friendship; but, when these are passed, there remains nothing to continue the work. A black pall falls between the past and the future, and strives to cover the very memory of bygone school years. Money, influence, position, make havoc, striving in the freest land to set up classes and aristocracies separated from what is common by impass-able barriers,--as though there were any other aristocracy than that of character and personal worth!

Ought girls to have intimate friends? How carelessly we use that word "inti-mate." Well, this is a very trying question, and needs a careful answer. Says Mr. Alger, "School-girl friendships are a proverb in all mouths. They form one of the largest classes of those human attachments whose idealizing power and sympathet-ic interfusions glorify the world, and sweeten existence. With what quick trust and ardor, what eager relish, these susceptible creatures, before whom heavenly illu-sions float, surrender themselves to each other, taste all the raptures of confidential conversation, lift veil after veil, till every secret is bare, and, hand in hand, with glowing feet, tread the paths of Paradise!" But what do you mean by "intimate"? If you understand by that word entire confidence in another under all circumstances; an unbosoming of every thought and feeling; a complete surrender to your friend, or mastery over her; a slavish adoration of her, and hearty concordance in all she does,--do not, then, indulge in an intimate friendship. The majority of women who have passed middle life will utter, out of their own experience, the truth that such confidence, such intercourse and familiarity, cause regret; and that such friendships are seriously detrimental to human happiness, wearing the mind, grieving the spirit; they cannot continue for many years. Our elders go even beyond that, and say that woman cannot love woman as woman can love man. Why is it that the friendships of boys usually last longer than those of girls? I cannot believe it is because girls are less constant or less friendly: I know they **are** not. Can it be because boys are less sensitive, and more sufficient for themselves? or is it because they are less intense, less confidential, and move along more slowly and suspiciously? Does it ever come from peculiarity of temperament in the case of both boys and girls, there being girl-boys and boy-girls? I am inclined to think that, because a boy is a boy, and a girl is a girl, the characteristics of both are required to make a perfect friendship. Of course there are broad exceptions to this opinion.

Can you have more than one intimate friend among the girls? That depends, too, on the nature and degree of closeness in the friendship. It requires a large amount of generosity on the part of several when two persons are close friends of a third. That blissful "*solitude a deux*" becomes misery *a trois*. The world is indeed beautiful, and the best part of it all is the people in it. We are to love as many of them as we can, but are called upon to reveal our inmost selves to few, very few, friends.

Valuing friendship more than any other earthly blessing, I think it wrong for girls to encourage that moodiness which flatters them they can do without friends, especially of their own sex. Nothing can conduce more to happiness: nothing is brighter, more charming, more helpful than the interchange of friendship among young women. Who wouldn't be a girl always if she could be sure all the other girls would stay so too, and go on in that delightful exchange of affection and fine feeling which is the very ecstacy of living?

Now, what does a girl prize most in another girl whose friendship she enjoys? or, rather, what should she value in her most? In the first place, constancy,--a knowledge that her friend will always be hers; and then honesty,--a feeling that, if she says, "Now, don't you tell," the friend won't tell. By the way, this binding to secrecy is a very bad practice, however delightful. It places too great a responsibility on one's friend, leads her into temptation, makes her curious, and, in nine times out of ten, one has no right to tell one's self, or one would not be so cautious.

Honesty implies more than this, however: it demands that your friend shall not herald abroad your mistakes or improprieties, though she may disapprove of them. It means that she shall treat you with the same kindness on all occasions, and that she shall resent wrong done you by another.

You like a girl who does not criticise unjustly, nor gossip about her friends. Marcus Aurelius, in his meditations, says, "A man must learn a great deal to enable him to pass a correct judgment on another man's acts." And Arthur Helps, in his essay, "On the Art of Living with Others," exclaims, "If you would be loved as a companion, avoid unnecessary criticism upon those with whom you live." Gossip is a most dangerous kind of criticism.

You prize a girl, too, who can like you even when she is not fond of your surroundings. An honest friendship does away with all jealousy, and makes each proud of the other's acquirements. "I must feel pride in my friend's accomplishments as if they were mine, and a property in his virtue."[7]

Girls are not sufficiently inclined to help girls. Think of the shadows which cross your path which some dear girl's hand could chase away. You would not drive the bird from your window-sill when he daily comes for crumbs, nor let a kitten stand mewing in the cold. Do not withhold the charity of your friendship from the hungry, dreary girl who waits. When the helping hands and generous hearts of such benefactors as every city knows,--women whose names are familiar to us as synonyms of charity, wisdom, rightness, but whose names we here repress because publicity would detract from the modesty of their conduct,--when such women stretch out hands of benefaction to their poor, ignorant, wicked sisters in our great towns, sparing something from their purses, from their minds, from their comforts, we wonder what must be the gift of their friendship to their more immediate friends. Here and there we meet humbler women, girls of fair intelligence and generous hearts, who give of their leisure, when they have no money, to help all objects of moral or spiritual wealth to woman. What must their friendship be to their friends! Something of immense value. Would there were more such engaged in a like work for the spreading of this broad friendship among women as women.

When a girl finds something of friendliness to give, the objects of her favor find much to receive. A blessing increases most rapidly while passing from possessor to recipient. The highest endowments should not, and do not, shut out a real need of reciprocal friendship in the hearts of girls. The larger your natures are, the greater will be your demand for friends. Do not be afraid you have not the talent of being friendly, even to the most gifted. A woman's greatest need, if she will confess it, is large-hearted sympathy,--is friendship. That one who withholds it, who seeks not friends, is fighting against herself, is lonely and dreary, notwithstanding the fact that she has great capabilities; for one of the most essential elements of her nature is being starved. The mightiest cannot stand alone. Mme. Swetchine, Marian Evans, Mme. De Stael felt, even more than most women, the absolute need of a friend. I can imagine nothing drearier than to be so far superior, in mind or in position, to one's associates as to feel no friendship for them. Milton, sitting with his daughters, yet not comprehended, is to me one of the saddest pictures of a great mental endowment and an unsatisfied heart. Would not Elizabeth have given years of her life and

---

7   Emerson

reign for the possession of one true friend? It is an extremely rare thing to hear of a woman hermit, or recluse. Girls give themselves up to nunneries, and believe they shut out the world; but they are either seeking the friendship of a cause supremely, or are hugging the closer an earthly, though a disappointed, love.

It is not weak, as Grace Aguilar suggests, for women to love women, girls to love girls. "It is the fashion to deride female friendship, to look with scorn on those who profess it. There is always, to me, a doubt of the warmth, the strength, and purity of her feelings, when a girl merges into womanhood, looking down on female friendship as romance and folly."

It makes no difference who you are, girls, you need friends among all classes and ages of persons. Sometimes it is the little child who can give friendship best; sometimes it is the woman bowed with years; often it is she whose years, surpassing yours by ten or twelve, have brought her into the midst of that experience on which you are just entering. Surely you must always need the sweet exchange of feeling which takes place between girls and girls.

We remark the countless friends we have in Nature; but beautiful, ennobling and comforting as the trees, the streams, and long green meadows are, you cannot afford to give up flesh and blood friends for them. Nature can improve you, but you cannot help her; but the true value of friendship is the mutual benefit to be derived from it.

In the highest sense, this benefit relates not only to the heart, but to the mind and soul. It is indeed possible for the ignorant, the unambitious, the unrefined to be firm friends. We hear of true and lasting friendships existing in peasant life. The rough, barren mountain-ways of the Scotch Highlands, the coast villages of France, the vinelands of Germany, the low flats of Holland, the desert of Africa, the vast plains of America, have furnished the most pathetic examples of sincere friendship, even though found among the most uncivilized. Surely, when refinement is added, the blessing should increase and not diminish, as it so often seems to do. The wigwam of the Indian is a truer protection for friendship than the gilded walls of many a drawing-room.

Oh, girls, this is what hurts and soils your characters,--this drawing- room insincerity, this falseness, this seeming! You can be polite and honest too; agreeable, and faithful as well. Significant glances, unfair advantages, uncivil pretensions in the parlor, make you not only insincere, but suspicious that you, also, are being ogled and scanned by others. Girls have contributed to make society false when they might have made it true. That society is insincere to you you will hardly deny, if poverty, sickness, or any misfortune thrust you from it. But society we must have. Why not, then, do your part to make it nobler, friendlier, truer? Much depends on the effort every girl makes to improve the social condition of the community.

Though you are so often indiscreet, fickle, ungenerous in your friendships, girls, I believe in them. When I see a party of you come together, so glad to be with one another again, giving and taking, after the most lavish fashion, I want to say, "Yes, indeed!" to Mr. Alger's remarks about school-girls; though I would leave off the word school, and make his expressions apply to girls everywhere. "Probably no chapter of sentiment in modern fashionable life is so intense and rich as that which comes to the experience of budding maidens at school. In their mental caresses, spiritual nuptials, their thoughts kiss each, other, and more than all the blessedness the world will ever give them is foreshadowed."

To sustain this friendship, I repeat, there are very necessary demands upon your patience, your charity, and your constancy. "The only way to have a friend is to be one," issues from the oracular lips of the Concord seer. "Men exist for the sake of one another. Teach them, or bear with them," is an appeal which has been handed down the ages from the wisdom of that great "seeker after God," Marcus Aurelius.

Next to constancy in our fondness for others should come forbearance and conformity. We ought to forbear inflicting the discomfort of our peculiarities on our friends, or of requiring too much love for what we give,--too much intelligence to meet our mental acquirements. We should forbear asking for a change of opinion, or an unsettling of conviction, and certainly should refrain from making a bad use of our intimacy with one another. Be deaf and dumb and blind to all attempts to draw from you the secrets which another has committed to your charge. Conformity is no less important than forbearance. We should adapt ourselves more to the tastes, habits, and dispositions of our friends. Of course, we are not to comply with what will work them and us harm. Girls agree to certain customs in the main; dress as their mates do; and, if this or that fashion prevails, follow it, when it is not too ridiculous,--perhaps some do even when it is absurd. When the majority of girls wear bangs and bangles, you wear them; and when the most wear skirts somewhat less than two yards around, why, I suppose you do, don't you? That is all right; but let it never be forgotten that, in conforming to general usage, you may still preserve your own personality. When bustles and French heels jostle with your individuality, let them go, but save yourselves.

How is it we so easily follow after fashion and custom, suffer physical and mental pangs on account of them, and yet find it so hard to conform with the notions and individual traits of our friends? Just here, however, we are reminded that we are not to so agree with our friends, even, as to lose ourselves. Says Arthur Helps on this point, "If it were not for some singular people who persist in thinking for themselves, in seeing for themselves, and in being comfortable, we should all collapse into a hideous uniformity.... In all things, a man must beware of so conforming himself as to crush his nature, and forego the purpose of his being." And Emerson might have added to that thought, "Better be a nettle in the side of your friend than his echo."

Conformity enjoins compromise. Fewer would be the great national calamities of war, famine, hard times; fewer the domestic trials; fewer the broken hearts, were there more of compromise in the world,--were there less cultivation and indulgence of certain national or personal peculiarities.

Girls ought never to be so familiar with one another as to forget to be polite in their intercourse. Courtesy, the last best gift of chivalry, the one bright star of the Middle Ages, leads out a long array of thoughts; but we cannot stop to marshal them here. Politeness is never superfluous. It needs to become so much a part of the costume of character as never to be laid aside except for renewal. Surely we should show its brightest ornaments, and the durability of its fabric, to our friends and acquaintances.

Let us seek friends, not wait for them to come to us. Let us search for them, not with boldness and indiscrimination, but with a hearty good-will to help them and enjoy them, as we, in return, expect them to do us good, and be glad of us. It is a duty on our part to seek and to keep friends, and no occupation should be so absolutely engrossing as to prevent the performance of this duty.

XI.
YOUTHS AND MAIDENS.

I have discovered an incompleteness, girls, in my talk with you about your friends, and I feel very depressing qualms of conscience on account of my discovery. Why, I haven't said one word about the friendships of boys and girls. Do pardon me! There really is an excuse. The fact is,--shall I speak it right out loud? No, it might be too dreadful. Come close, girls, and I will whisper it in your ears,--I am an old maid! Isn't that deplorable? I have lost one-half the pleasure there is in friendship, and, perhaps, you think, all there is in love. Yes, 'tis true: I am one of the superfluous sixty thousand women who are usurping the population in a small state. I had better go to the far West, and settle in the gold diggings, hadn't I?

So, girls, you do not suppose that, in a condition of such positive ignorance, I am able to talk with you about the boys? Well, I will be very discreet, and only suppose, gently suppose, that such a thing as friendship exists among boys and girls. But if I should venture on the subject of marriage, which, I am told, often ensues from something akin to friendship, you will please pardon me, and remember that, if I am too old to be talking about it, you are too young to be listening.

In such a peculiar civilization as ours, you cannot be really getting married at eighteen. But you may be thinking about marriage. Oh, yes! girls think a great deal about it at that age. Perhaps I did when I was eighteen; but that was so long ago, so very long ago! Still, for present purposes, we will imagine I was once a girl, and thought more or less about the boys, and liked them, too, just as you do now.

Oh, do not be so sure, you very bashful or very independent few, that you do not care a fig for the boys, and never shall! If you feel a kind of indifference now, or cannot see what boys are for, unless to try their sisters, and act conceited and foolish with the other girls, you may be on the verge of discovering that they are extremely good for loving.

Isn't it remarkable how boys change? Why, you are so suddenly impressed that Tom Sydney is not half as rude as he used to be! Indeed, he has grown very polite,--he lifts his hat in such a deferential way; he speaks with so manly a tone; he has a touch of such gentlemanly, half- alluring kindness when he helps you over the crossing! Strange, one's neighbors do alter so! Yes, it is a little remarkable; but it is on both sides of the street,--girls as well as boys.

It is not the freshman year in college, nor the first month in business, nor the first term at an evening dancing-school, which produce the change in the boys. It is not graduation, nor parties, nor house-keeping responsibilities, which make such a change in girls. No; but it is a very beautiful unfolding of the decrees of God which makes boys and girls love one another.

But, girls, even if your mind is set on celibacy, and you feel able to set off by contrasting charms the bliss of matrimony, encourage the friendship of the boys. You need their friendliness just as they need yours. You require their steadiness of purpose, their decision, their frankness, their slower judgment, their more robust endeavor, their courage and hardihood. They need your keener perception of right and wrong, your forbearance, your refinement of feeling, your encouragement, your sympathy, your patience and endurance, your tact, your gentleness and grace. The boys, you see, have the advantage of giving you more than you can give them; and you have the advantage of imparting to them more than they can impart to you. And, pray, what is friendship but a mutual giving and taking of the best parts of character? And how, indeed, can boys and girls grow in character without friends? Do not fancy the boys like in you qualities differing from those the girls are most fond of. Very young boys may, or very unworthy men. A twelve-year-old thinks girls are "no good,"--can't fly a kite without letting go the string, and can't play ball without hitting him on the head with a bat. A fifteen-year-old thinks girls will do for some occasions, especially if the girls are his sisters. They can fasten neck-ties very well, and save a fellow a good deal of embarrassment at dancing-school. He wishes they wouldn't be such tell- tales, though. But an eighteen-year-old, or a youth of twenty, cannot conceive any thing more adorable than the winning ways of girlhood.

A boy likes a girl sometimes, just as you girls too often like each other, because she is pretty, or bright, or pert. He is fond of a girl at other times because the beauty of her character reveals itself in all kinds of womanly acts. If he marries, he usually meets the deserts of whatever fondness he cherishes. He may be happy for a while in association with a pretty face, a saucy tongue, and a becoming costume; but not for long,--not for long.

While you are never to forget that you are young women, and that you owe large tributes to girls everywhere, do not exact consideration from the boys merely because you are girls. The boys never think of asking you to favor them. Though you are privileged to demand courtesy, that should not prevent you from engaging in honest toil with boys, or from associating with them in harmless pleasures. A boy appreciates it when a girl takes hold and helps to row, to rake, or to add accounts.

I think it is extremely commendable when a boy and girl can study together, work in the factory at the same bench, drive or walk with one another, and are not foolishly conscious that he is a boy and she is a girl. It is a pleasure to see a girl look at a boy without blushing, and to observe a boy look into a girl's eyes without immediately lowering his lashes.

Why is this susceptibility? It is not because boys and girls are always to fall in love when they meet. Every girl has a work to do for the boys,--some traits in their characters to discountenance, some features to encourage. How can she do this, if she is always thinking, Maybe he loves me? Work with the boys she must: join in merry-making and in whimsical enjoyments, why should she not? but in her gayest moment let her be mindful, not of a difference in sex, but of the fact that both a boy and a girl owe deference to each other, courtesy, kindness, and conformity, as of friend with friend.

It is quite possible for young women to have friends among the young men without this friendship developing into a strong affection. You do not know, girls, how valiantly you are defended by the boys. Boys are usually such uncommunicative creatures! But touch their friendship, and they will throw a volley of rhetoric right in among a crowd of gossipers. Slow to receive favors from you, as they sometimes seem, they never forget a kindness done by you.

Now suppose your association with boys does sometime grow into a love for a young man,--just suppose the case. Ought you to marry him? Of course I don't know: I am not capable of advising, on account of my singularity. I might tremblingly suggest, however, that love, health, and virtue having been seriously contemplated, there should be few, if any, hindrances to marriage; for out of this trinity will spring patience, courage, industry, joy, and all that is needful to united lives.

If you think my suggestion lacks the significance of experience, why, hunt up some of the best authorities on the subject. William Penn was a very moral kind of a man, and experienced in the art of living; and, like a true Quaker, he put a negative wherever one was needed. He said, "Never marry but for love, but see thou lovest what is lovely." Only two conditions, you note; but on them hangs the destiny of all the future. It is certainly right for you to think of marriage, to regard it joyfully, yet so as with a serious joy. But girls, dear girls, do not inflame your hearts with the visions of married life which are so frequently delineated in the prevalent fiction of the day. You will be happier without all that extravagance of romantic affection which fills circulating libraries. Do not read the trash: it will make you expect too much; it will make real life seem insignificant; it will cause you to be more and more susceptible in the presence of young men; it will blot leaves in your book of life which ought to be all white; it will make truth fictitious; it will lead to temptation,--to death. Says Miss Yonge, "If every modest woman or girl would abstain from such books as poison, and never order or read one which makes crime and impurity prominent, or tampers with dilemmas about the marriage vow, there would be fewer written and published, and less wildfire would be spread abroad." Shun the romances which centre all in a false, unnatural affection. Oh, that they were all sunk in the ocean, the food for obscene sharks! And, oh, that only such pure and beautiful romances remained as picture the lives of a Hermann and a Dorothea, or a Gabriel and an Evangeline!

But, girls, how some of you do treat the boys! No wonder they grow conceited: you allow them to become so. Here is a girl only eighteen years old who has an impression, such a strong impression, there is but one praise-worthy act for a girl to do, and that is to get married. Each new birthday will frighten her, and she will dread to be alive and single at twenty-five. She seizes every matrimonial opportunity, and haunts a young man like a conviction of conscience.

Here is another girl quite absorbed in the thought that a *live* man pays her certain attentions, and she takes his conceit for grave wisdom, and his kindness for infinite tenderness. She looks upon him as an importation from the priesthood of

the Grand Llama,--perhaps he is the Grand Llama himself; certainly the inhabit-
ant of a land where young men do not grow humanly. He is a ***rara avis***, a glorious
phenomenon, a marked consideration in the world, a being to be devoutly gazed at
to come to some appreciation of him.

I feel you are berating me, girls, so far as your natures will allow; but, then, do
I not speak the truth? Could I not unfold pitiful stories about girls who marry fine
wedding receptions and the servitude of reverses? about young women who are
vain enough to think there can be no union of hearts without union of intellects,
and so lay snares for college students? Could I not picture to you the ***mariage de
convenance*** in America? And could I not describe the marriage of a jilt?

I cannot too earnestly repeat that marriage is the common and acceptable destiny of both boys and girls; but I must complain because girls do not regard it sufficiently before they enter into it. In the distress which follows their hastiness, in
the despair which sometimes hardens their hearts, women call marriage a lottery,
and man faithless.

I must think that marriage is not only a very natural, but a very beautiful, way
of increasing love.

"Love is the burden of all Nature's odes,--the song of the birds an epithala-
mium, a hymeneal. The marriage of the flowers spots the meadows, and fringes the
hedges with pearls and diamonds. In the deep waters, in the high air, in woods and
pastures, and the bowels of the earth, this is the employment and condition of all
things."[8]

"God has set the type of marriage everywhere throughout the creation. Each
creature seeks its perfection in another. The very heavens and earth picture it to
us."[9]

Youths and maidens, you are in the heyday of vigorous, joyous life! Your delight is, like the springtime, rich in hope and promise. Your laugh rings true; your
voices mingle in frolic glee, or in quiet tones of kind regard. Now join hands in the
glad though earnest work of life,--not life's drudgery, not its toils. No! for the cheer
of your spirits, the courage which looks despair full in the face, and crushes it with
lively endeavor,--these will permit no drudgery; these will make out of the most

8   Thoreau
9   Luther

desolate moorland a very garden of life!

You can do *all*! Now make the earth renew its vigor; now make health and courage come again in the world; now restore the reign of cheer; now break the bonds of vice; now bring back an earthly Paradise! With your strong bodies, your glad hearts, your vigorous minds, your imperial sway over the hearts of one another, your persuasive control over the feelings of your elders, it is for you to make the future what you will. Oh, make it the dawn of that civilization, of that Christianity, when again "the morning stars shall sing together!"

Only you can restore virtue; only you can cast out corruption; only you can drive the fiends of intemperance, of fraud, of oppression, of despair, of craftiness, of selfishness, from the land!

Girls, in the great work of the future, in the reformation of the present, can you not do most? When woman was thrust out of Paradise, man followed her. When she shall return again, and the gates shall swing open on noiseless hinges at the approach of her pure feet, man shall be seen, not following, but walking by her side.

Raphael and Guido have painted the angel Michael with a beautiful maiden's face, though his body is muscular, and his wings are tipped with strength, while, firm as a Hercules, he stands upon the writhing coils of Satan. The Devil but turns his coward head to look with vanquished strength upon the clear, calm smile of the angel. Maidenly love of what is pure, of what is brave, of what is manly, will crush the evil in youths who are tempted; yes, and make from an Adam of mere muscle and intelligence a very god of virtue.

The Codes Of Hammurabi And Moses
W. W. Davies

QTY

The discovery of the Hammurabi Code is one of the greatest achievements of archaeology, and is of paramount interest, not only to the student of the Bible, but also to all those interested in ancient history...

Religion   **ISBN: *1-59462-338-4***   **Pages:132**

MSRP $12.95

The Theory of Moral Sentiments
Adam Smith

QTY

This work from 1749. contains original theories of conscience amd moral judgment and it is the foundation for systemof morals.

Philosophy **ISBN: *1-59462-777-0***   **Pages:536**

MSRP $19.95

Jessica's First Prayer
Hesba Stretton

QTY

In a screened and secluded corner of one of the many railway-bridges which span the streets of London there could be seen a few years ago, from five o'clock every morning until half past eight, a tidily set-out coffee-stall, consisting of a trestle and board, upon which stood two large tin cans, with a small fire of charcoal burning under each so as to keep the coffee boiling during the early hours of the morning when the work-people were thronging into the city on their way to their daily toil...

Childrens   **ISBN: *1-59462-373-2***

Pages:84

MSRP $9.95

My Life and Work
Henry Ford

QTY

Henry Ford revolutionized the world with his implementation of mass production for the Model T automobile. Gain valuable business insight into his life and work with his own auto-biography... "We have only started on our development of our country we have not as yet, with all our talk of wonderful progress, done more than scratch the surface. The progress has been wonderful enough but..."

Biographies/   **ISBN: *1-59462-198-5***

Pages:300

MSRP $21.95

The Art of Cross-Examination
Francis Wellman

I presume it is the experience of every author, after his first book is published upon an important subject, to be almost overwhelmed with a wealth of ideas and illustrations which could readily have been included in his book, and which to his own mind, at least, seem to make a second edition inevitable. Such certainly was the case with me; and when the first edition had reached its sixth impression in five months, I rejoiced to learn that it seemed to my publishers that the book had met with a sufficiently favorable reception to justify a second and considerably enlarged edition. ..

Pages:412

Reference   **ISBN:** *1-59462-647-2*   *MSRP $19.95*

QTY

On the Duty of Civil Disobedience
Henry David Thoreau

Thoreau wrote his famous essay, On the Duty of Civil Disobedience, as a protest against an unjust but popular war and the immoral but popular institution of slave-owning. He did more than write—he declined to pay his taxes, and was hauled off to gaol in consequence. Who can say how much this refusal of his hastened the end of the war and of slavery ?

Law   **ISBN:** *1-59462-747-9*

Pages:48

MSRP $7.45

QTY

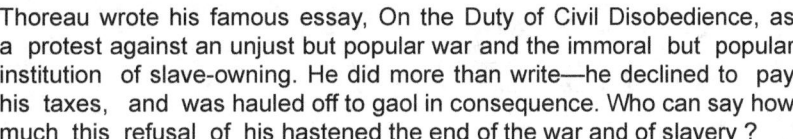

Dream Psychology Psychoanalysis for Beginners
Sigmund Freud

Sigmund Freud, born Sigismund Schlomo Freud (May 6, 1856 - September 23, 1939), was a Jewish-Austrian neurologist and psychiatrist who co-founded the psychoanalytic school of psychology. Freud is best known for his theories of the unconscious mind, especially involving the mechanism of repression; his redefinition of sexual desire as mobile and directed towards a wide variety of objects; and his therapeutic techniques, especially his understanding of transference in the therapeutic relationship and the presumed value of dreams as sources of insight into unconscious desires.

Pages:196

Psychology   **ISBN:** *1-59462-905-6*   *MSRP $15.45*

QTY

The Miracle of Right Thought
Orison Swett Marden

Believe with all of your heart that you will do what you were made to do. When the mind has once formed the habit of holding cheerful, happy, prosperous pictures, it will not be easy to form the opposite habit. It does not matter how improbable or how far away this realization may see, or how dark the prospects may be, if we visualize them as best we can, as vividly as possible, hold tenaciously to them and vigorously struggle to attain them, they will gradually become actualized, realized in the life. But a desire, a longing without endeavor, a yearning abandoned or held indifferently will vanish without realization.

Pages:360

Self Help   **ISBN:** *1-59462-644-8*   *MSRP $25.45*

QTY

QTY

The Rosicrucian Cosmo-Conception Mystic Christianity by *Max Heindel*   ISBN: *1-59462-188-8* **$38.95**
The Rosicrucian Cosmo-conception is not dogmatic, neither does it appeal to any other authority than the reason of the student. It is: not controversial, but is: sent forth in the, hope that it may help to clear...   New Age/Religion Pages 646

Abandonment To Divine Providence by *Jean-Pierre de Caussade*   ISBN: *1-59462-228-0* **$25.95**
"The Rev. Jean Pierre de Caussade was one of the most remarkable spiritual writers of the Society of Jesus in France in the 18th Century. His death took place at Toulouse in 1751. His works have gone through many editions and have been republished...   Inspirational/Religion Pages 400

Mental Chemistry by *Charles Haanel*   ISBN: *1-59462-192-6* **$23.95**
Mental Chemistry allows the change of material conditions by combining and appropriately utilizing the power of the mind. Much like applied chemistry creates something new and unique out of careful combinations of chemicals the mastery of mental chemistry...   New Age Pages 354

The Letters of Robert Browning and Elizabeth Barret Barrett 1845-1846 vol II   ISBN: *1-59462-193-4* **$35.95**
by *Robert Browning* and *Elizabeth Barrett*   Biographies Pages 596

Gleanings In Genesis (volume I) by *Arthur W. Pink*   ISBN: *1-59462-130-6* **$27.45**
Appropriately has Genesis been termed "the seed plot of the Bible" for in it we have, in germ form, almost all of the great doctrines which are afterwards fully developed in the books of Scripture which follow...   Religion/Inspirational Pages 420

The Master Key by *L. W. de Laurence*   ISBN: *1-59462-001-6* **$30.95**
In no branch of human knowledge has there been a more lively increase of the spirit of research during the past few years than in the study of Psychology, Concentration and Mental Discipline. The requests for authentic lessons in Thought Control, Mental Discipline and...   New Age/Business Pages 422

The Lesser Key Of Solomon Goetia by *L. W. de Laurence*   ISBN: *1-59462-092-X* **$9.95**
This translation of the first book of the "Lernegton" which is now for the first time made accessible to students of Talismanic Magic was done, after careful collation and edition, from numerous Ancient Manuscripts in Hebrew, Latin, and French...   New Age/Occult Pages 92

Rubaiyat Of Omar Khayyam by *Edward Fitzgerald*   ISBN: *1-59462-332-5* **$13.95**
Edward Fitzgerald, whom the world has already learned, in spite of his own efforts to remain within the shadow of anonymity, to look upon as one of the rarest poets of the century, was born at Bredfield, in Suffolk, on the 31st of March, 1809. He was the third son of John Purcell...   Music Pages 172

Ancient Law by *Henry Maine*   ISBN: *1-59462-128-4* **$29.95**
The chief object of the following pages is to indicate some of the earliest ideas of mankind, as they are reflected in Ancient Law, and to point out the relation of those ideas to modern thought.   Religiom/History Pages 452

Far-Away Stories by *William J. Locke*   ISBN: *1-59462-129-2* **$19.45**
"Good wine needs no bush, but a collection of mixed vintages does. And this book is just such a collection. Some of the stories I do not want to remain buried for ever in the museum files of dead magazine-numbers an author's not unpardonable vanity..."   Fiction Pages 272

Life of David Crockett by *David Crockett*   ISBN: *1-59462-250-7* **$27.45**
"Colonel David Crockett was one of the most remarkable men of the times in which he lived. Born in humble life, but gifted with a strong will, an indomitable courage, and unremitting perseverance...   Biographies/New Age Pages 424

Lip-Reading by *Edward Nitchie*   ISBN: *1-59462-206-X* **$25.95**
Edward B. Nitchie, founder of the New York School for the Hard of Hearing, now the Nitchie School of Lip-Reading, Inc, wrote "LIP-READING Principles and Practice". The development and perfecting of this meritorious work on lip-reading was an undertaking...   How-to Pages 400

A Handbook of Suggestive Therapeutics, Applied Hypnotism, Psychic Science   ISBN: *1-59462-214-0* **$24.95**
by *Henry Munro*   Health/New Age/Health/Self-help Pages 376

A Doll's House: and Two Other Plays by *Henrik Ibsen*   ISBN: *1-59462-112-8* **$19.95**
Henrik Ibsen created this classic when in revolutionary 1848 Rome. Introducing some striking concepts in playwriting for the realist genre, this play has been studied the world over.   Fiction/Classics/Plays 308

The Light of Asia by *sir Edwin Arnold*   ISBN: *1-59462-204-3* **$13.95**
In this poetic masterpiece, Edwin Arnold describes the life and teachings of Buddha. The man who was to become known as Buddha to the world was born as Prince Gautama of India but he rejected the worldly riches and abandoned the reigns of power when...   Religion/History/Biographies Pages 170

The Complete Works of Guy de Maupassant by *Guy de Maupassant*   ISBN: *1-59462-157-8* **$16.95**
"For days and days, nights and nights, I had dreamed of that first kiss which was to consecrate our engagement, and I knew not on what spot I should put my lips..."   Fiction/Classics Pages 240

The Art of Cross-Examination by *Francis L. Wellman*   ISBN: *1-59462-309-0* **$26.95**
Written by a renowned trial lawyer, Wellman imparts his experience and uses case studies to explain how to use psychology to extract desired information through questioning.   How-to/Science/Reference Pages 408

Answered or Unanswered? by *Louisa Vaughan*   ISBN: *1-59462-248-5* **$10.95**
Miracles of Faith in China   Religion Pages 112

The Edinburgh Lectures on Mental Science (1909) by *Thomas*   ISBN: *1-59462-008-3* **$11.95**
This book contains the substance of a course of lectures recently given by the writer in the Queen Street Hail, Edinburgh. Its purpose is to indicate the Natural Principles governing the relation between Mental Action and Material Conditions...   New Age/Psychology Pages 148

Ayesha by *H. Rider Haggard*   ISBN: *1-59462-301-5* **$24.95**
Verily and indeed it is the unexpected that happens! Probably if there was one person upon the earth from whom the Editor of this, and of a certain previous history, did not expect to hear again...   Classics Pages 380

Ayala's Angel by *Anthony Trollope*   ISBN: *1-59462-352-X* **$29.95**
The two girls were both pretty, but Lucy who was twenty-one who supposed to be simple and comparatively unattractive, whereas Ayala was credited, as her Bombwhat romantic name might show, with poetic charm and a taste for romance. Ayala when her father died was nineteen...   Fiction Pages 484

The American Commonwealth by *James Bryce*   ISBN: *1-59462-286-8* **$34.45**
An interpretation of American democratic political theory. It examines political mechanics and society from the perspective of Scotsman James Bryce   Politics Pages 572

Stories of the Pilgrims by *Margaret P. Pumphrey*   ISBN: *1-59462-116-0* **$17.95**
This book explores pilgrims religious oppression in England as well as their escape to Holland and eventual crossing to America on the Mayflower, and their early days in New England...   History Pages 268

QTY

The Fasting Cure *by Sinclair Upton*   ISBN: *1-59462-222-1* **$13.95**

In the Cosmopolitan Magazine for May, 1910, and in the Contemporary Review (London) for April, 1910, I published an article dealing with my experiences in fasting. I have written a great many magazine articles, but never one which attracted so much attention... New Age/Self Help/Health Pages 164

Hebrew Astrology *by Sepharial*   ISBN: *1-59462-308-2* **$13.45**

In these days of advanced thinking it is a matter of common observation that we have left many of the old landmarks behind and that we are now pressing forward to greater heights and to a wider horizon than that which represented the mind-content of our progenitors... Astrology Pages 144

Thought Vibration or The Law of Attraction in the Thought World   ISBN: *1-59462-127-6* **$12.95**

by William Walker Atkinson   *Psychology/Religion Pages 144*

Optimism *by Helen Keller*   ISBN: *1-59462-108-X* **$15.95**

Helen Keller was blind, deaf, and mute since 19 months old, yet famously learned how to overcome these handicaps, communicate with the world, and spread her lectures promoting optimism. An inspiring read for everyone... Biographies/Inspirational Pages 84

Sara Crewe *by Frances Burnett*   ISBN: *1-59462-360-0* **$9.45**

In the first place, Miss Minchin lived in London. Her home was a large, dull, tall one, in a large, dull square, where all the houses were alike, and all the sparrows were alike, and where all the door-knockers made the same heavy sound... Childrens/Classic Pages 88

The Autobiography of Benjamin Franklin *by Benjamin Franklin*   ISBN: *1-59462-135-7* **$24.95**

The Autobiography of Benjamin Franklin has probably been more extensively read than any other American historical work, and no other book of its kind has had such ups and downs of fortune. Franklin lived for many years in England, where he was agent... Biographies/History Pages 332

Name	
Email	
Telephone	
Address	
City, State ZIP	

☐ **Credit Card**   ☐ **Check / Money Order**

Credit Card Number	
Expiration Date	
Signature	

Please Mail to: *Book Jungle*
PO Box 2226
Champaign, IL 61825
or Fax to: *630-214-0564*

ORDERING INFORMATION

web: *www.bookjungle.com*
email: *sales@bookjungle.com*
fax: *630-214-0564*
mail: *Book Jungle PO Box 2226 Champaign, IL 61825*
or PayPal *to sales@bookjungle.com*

Please contact us for bulk discounts

DIRECT-ORDER TERMS

**20% Discount if You Order
Two or More Books**
Free Domestic Shipping!
Accepted: Master Card, Visa,
Discover, American Express

www.ingramcontent.com/pod-product-compliance
Lightning Source LLC
Chambersburg PA
CBHW082016170626
46817CB00009B/3106